A KING FOR THE SORCERESS

THE DRAGONS OF FIRE AND ICE

BOOK TWO

AMELIA SHAW

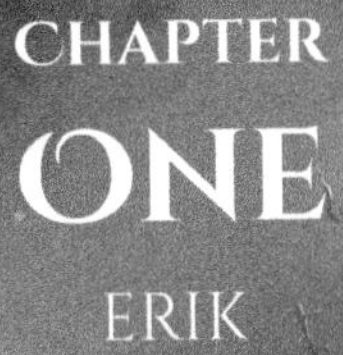

CHAPTER
ONE

ERIK

I knelt with my head bowed, every word the elder spoke placing the weight of the world on my shoulders.

"Bravadik Arman. Son of Sigmus, King of the Black Mountains. I anoint you and bestow upon you the kingdom and clan of your father. In your hands, I place responsibility, duty, and power. May this crown grow into a symbol of your strength. May you rise to be the leader your blood rite destines you to become."

I suppressed the shudder that passed through me. I'd dreaded this moment since the day my mother told me the name of my true sire. He had been the last person in the kingdom I expected. *The king.*

"Arise, King Bravadik," the elder said, startling me out of my reflections. I took a long deep breath before pushing to my feet and turning to face the room full of courtiers and honored guests, people who had traveled for the coronation ceremony of the new king. *Me.*

Cheers and applause rang through the room. The guests were on their feet, shouting for me. Praising me. They were all people I'd never seen before. People I didn't know.

My mother was gone. She had died the past winter, having been ill for many years.

Pain squeezed my chest at the thought of her, as though someone had reached inside my ribs and grasped hold of my heart. If I tried, I could picture her standing in the crowd, looking up at me, her eyes shining with devotion and love. She would have been so proud to see me take the throne.

Despite the fact I never wanted it.

I still didn't. Not the throne, nor the castle. And especially not the kingdom.

Hordes of well-wishers surged forward to congratulate me and, despite my misgivings, I held my head high as I made my way down the stairs, clasping hands with the first man to step forward.

"King Bravadik, it is an honor," the man said, smiling broadly. He had a kind, open face, and I couldn't help but smile back.

I made my way through the crowd, greeting people here and there as they waved to me. Disappointment surged through me when I realized that my half-brother's queen wasn't here.

Queen Marienne.

Five years ago, I laid eyes on her for the first time.

The first, and the last.

The crowds before me parted, and a man emerged. With one look, I straightened my spine and lifted my chin to look him in the eye. All of my dragon shifter kinsmen were tall and broad, but there was no mistaking this man for a mere courtier.

"Your Highness," I said, bowing my head, at least until the man's laugh rolled through his chest, coming out deep and loud.

"You're a king now. You bow to no-one."

I raised my head. It would take time to get used to the fact that I was now a leader.

He reached out, offering me his hand. I recognized the

strength in his grip for the test that it was, and squeezed back, hard.

"Thank you for coming to the coronation," I said.

He grinned at me and pulled the woman next to him closer. Her breasts were so big and round they were practically toppling over the edge of her bodice.

"I'm Stavrok, King of Bravdok." His grin widened. "And this is my wife, Queen Lucy."

"Lucy?" I said, repeating the strange name.

She smiled, and her whole face lit up. "I'm not from around here."

My gaze slid back to Stavrok and I raised an eyebrow in question.

"I stole her." Stavrok grinned mischievously. "Out of the local village."

"The local... human village?" I was shocked by how casual they sounded.

"Yes," he said, puffing out his chest. "She'd never seen a dragon before me."

Lucy rolled her eyes, her expression fond. "It's very nice to meet you, Bravadik."

I scowled at the sound of my formal name. "My friends call me Erik."

Stavrok lifted his chin. A smirk tugged at his lips. "You have some of your father in you."

I took a step closer. "You knew him?"

Stavrok nodded. "Very well. Come to our castle for dinner one evening and we will discuss it at length. I've got plenty of old stories, if you wish to hear them?"

"I would appreciate that," I said, my voice rough with emotion. "Thank you."

"Come tomorrow night," Lucy said. "Bring Marienne with you. It has been too long since we've seen Mari. How is she?"

I made some low sound, deep in the back of my throat, and for some reason my dragon surged within my chest.

The mood shifted. Stavrok grabbed his wife and shoved her behind him, all the while rumbling out a growl that made my hackles rise and every muscle in my body clench to keep from shifting then and there.

What the hell?

My dragon was ferocious, sure. But my control was better than *this.*

"Get yourself together, or you're gonna force me to shift," Stavrok hissed through gritted teeth.

I caught a glimpse of his dragon in the way his nostrils flared, and the fire that burned in the depths of his gaze, and fought my own dragon's need to rise.

I clenched my fists until the knuckles whitened, trying to regain control.

Stavrok summoned a nearby male servant, who snapped to attention.

"A large glass of whiskey for King Bravadik. Now."

The servant dashed away. I forced myself to keep breathing in deep, even inhales and exhales.

Stavrok continued to hold Lucy back. The gorgeous little human fought against his arms, resolutely trying to peek around his barrel-like chest to get a look at me.

When the servant reappeared with the glass and a bottle, I ignored the glass and drank straight from the bottle, downing gulps. The whiskey burned my throat, all the way to my gut.

I swigged some more, and when that too reached my empty stomach, the need to shift finally began to subside.

My vision cleared and my shifter relaxed, yawning, and curling up to sleep inside me.

Stupid thing. We're trying to make a good impression, and you almost started a fight with our neighboring kingdom.

My self-anger must have shown on my face, because the servant took a couple of steps back like I was going to take a swing at him any moment.

"Thank you," I said belatedly.

The servant continued to stare at me with startled, wide eyes, not looking reassured in the slightest.

"Please, just..." I clutched the now half-empty bottle and waved him off. "You should leave."

I looked over at Stavrok, who allowed his little wife back around his huge body so that she could stare up at me with barely disguised curiosity.

"Did I say something wrong?" Lucy asked, then bit her lip in the sweetest way. "I'm still not sure about all the customs... Forgive me if I offended you."

I was too embarrassed to even *look* at her. "You did nothing wrong," I said stiffly, staring over her shoulder. Then I met Stavrok's gaze and inclined my head. "Thank you. That drink helped a lot."

Stavrok reached out and squeezed my shoulder. "We need to have that dinner sooner rather than later. Come tomorrow night, with or without Mari. No arguments."

"But..." Lucy began.

Stavrok gripped her hand and shook his head. "Marienne is the childless widow of the old king. She will not have a role in this kingdom unless the new king wishes it." His eyes found mine, narrowing. "If I were in his shoes, I would build a house somewhere at the edge of town and put her in it."

Stavrok's gaze intensified. I nodded and hummed as though agreeing.

Part of me could see his point. Marienne was part of the old court, the old ways. Her presence might divide loyalties.

Yes, sending her away would be the logical thing to do.

But the idea didn't sit right with me for a number of reasons, none of which, unfortunately, I could share in my present company.

"Where *is* Mari, by the way?" Lucy asked as she glanced around, scanning the crowd as if the woman might appear at any moment. "You haven't shipped her off already, have you?"

Mari. I liked the sound of the shortened name. Stavrok and Lucy obviously held an affection for my half-brother's widow, despite the fact that Stavrok had just urged me to ship her off.

I shook my head and lifted the bottle of whiskey, taking another sip to calm the way my frame was going rigid again.

"No." I looked down into the bottle, swirling around the liquid inside to avoid her gaze. "I wouldn't do such a thing."

"In that case..." Lucy's glare burned into the side of my head. I could feel it. "Where *is* she?"

I looked over toward Stavrok for support. "I would have assumed a human woman would be more malleable..."

Stavrok's bark of laughter was so loud, most of the people in the throne room turned to stare at us.

Lucy whacked him, and he calmed down a little, though nothing could pull the grin from his lips.

"No. Lucy is all fire." He looked down at her with pride. "Especially since giving birth to our triplets. She is the perfect mother dragon for my heirs."

"Triplets?" *Wow.*

My regard for the little human went up. Beauty, brains, and breeding. Stavrok had hit the perfect trifecta.

"Babies, Stavrok. We've talked about this. They are not simply... heirs." Lucy rolled her eyes.

"Our son *will* inherit the kingdom one day, my love."

I glanced between them with amusement. So, there seemed to be *some* cultural adjustments necessary when it came to human-dragon relationships.

Lucy huffed and puffed, apparently not having an argument

for that one. Then, she turned that icy stare back on me. "You didn't answer my question. Where's Marienne?"

I released a deep sigh.

"I don't know," I admitted. "When I arrived, the staff said she was in mourning and would not be attending my coronation. So…" I turned away from them a little, pretending intense interest in a nearby marble column. "I've left her alone. But I have to assume she's still in the castle somewhere. Hiding from me, it would seem."

I neglected to mention that I was hiding from *her,* as well. Nothing would have stopped me from chasing her down if I'd truly wanted to know where she was.

"Maybe she's in the dungeons," Lucy said under her breath, casting a sidelong look at her husband.

Did she just say *dungeons?* "Why would my half-brother's queen be in the dungeons?"

Stavrok shook his head. "That's a long story, my friend. We'll have to tell it to you some other time."

He glanced over his shoulder, at the line of people waiting for me. I suppressed another sigh.

"We will see you tomorrow night, Erik," Stavrok said. "Eight o'clock. Bring your appetite."

I shook the king's hand again. This time, his grip seemed friendlier.

"Thank you again for your help." I lifted the bottle to indicate the alcohol, giving him a sheepish smile. My head was slightly buzzing, and my stomach burned with liquor. But my control was back intact. "I apologize if my behavior scared you, or your lovely wife."

Stavrok chortled, a growly laugh that set my dragon on edge. "Erik, the only reason I didn't take your damn head off was because you obviously don't have much experience controlling your emotions. That has to change, and I'll be happy to help."

I gave the king a small smile, trying to remain calm. Rumor was that Stavrok had killed my half-brother in hand-to-hand combat. He was a tough warrior. Not one to cross, that was for sure.

"No hard feelings, then?" I asked.

As the king, I needed allies. And, despite his ferocity and loud, bombastic manner, I sensed that Stavrok had a good heart underneath.

Stavrok grinned. "As long as you stop staring at my wife's breasts… we're all good."

"Oh… of course," *Had* I been looking there?

My mind was still on Marienne—or Mari, as they had called her—and whether I should insist she come out of hiding.

Inadvertent staring at Stavrok's wife was likely just the first of many royal fuck-ups.

How many more would I have before my time was done?

TWO

MARIENNE

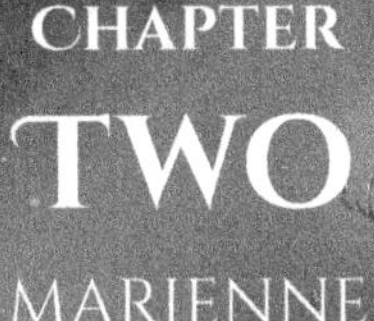

I watched my husband, King Magnik of the Black Mountains, die at the hand of another dragon king in mortal combat. It was by far the most traumatic day of my life.

It was also the most liberating.

From the moment my magic began to show itself, my destiny had been set in stone. I'd been all of sixteen at the time; I didn't know how to control my powers, and I couldn't hide them.

The power that stirred within me made me a worthy prize. I was to be a royal bride. My parents had fought to make the king wait until I was eighteen to claim me.

For ten long years, I'd been the queen of a clan ruled by a tyrant.

In the town below us, the distant chime of bells rang out. They were still celebrating, ringing in their new king.

The day of Magnik's half-brother's coronation had been a long time coming. Hope was in the air, and the entire kingdom felt it. The servants carried the rumors all the way to my tower. This king would be different. Not capricious and power-hungry like the last, and the one before that.

A shiver coursed through my body at the mere thought of Bravadik.

"Erik…" I whispered the more familiar name into the silence.

Only the wind answered me. The silken curtains fluttered, billowing outwards. I collapsed onto the nearby couch, reveling in the soft velvet cushions that surrounded me. This place was my oasis; it sheltered me from the pain of the world outside.

But I couldn't stay in here forever. Sooner or later, these walls would come crashing down and reality would intrude.

I had to be ready. I had to *think*.

With a small sigh, I rose from the couch and paced around my room. It was a cozy space, full of books and plush decorations. Colorful rugs covered the floor, and a large lantern hung from the ceiling, casting the furniture with a warm glow.

Magnik himself had told me of Bravadik, many years ago. His father's bastard son, and the only true challenger for the throne. He was low-born, the child of some village woman and known in his home town as Erik. He had been raised down in the valley, far away from court, and that was likely the only reason Magnik had not had him killed.

I'd seen Bravadik only once, on a royal tour, five years into my marriage. The moment stood out sharply in my memory. Even now, the thought of that day filled me with a cacophony of feelings. Happiness, love, and terror.

From the moment I lay eyes on Bravadik, I knew.

He was my fated mate.

It had been more than five years since that day. The day my heart broke in my chest when I knew we would never have the chance to be together.

The original joy I had felt when I saw Erik had been crushed mere seconds later. I could never know him. Nor love him.

I'd been forced to marry a man who had claimed me for my

magical power. Magnik was a distant, cold husband. He neither desired nor loved me. I was a tool to him, just another weapon in his arsenal.

The fates had cursed our union. My barren womb and untouched heart were a true testament to the emptiness of our marriage.

I turned my head toward the banging on the door, and called to whoever was on the other side. "I gave instructions that I don't wish to be disturbed."

"Queen Marienne."

My stomach dropped at the sound of the voice. I had never heard it before, and yet... I *knew* it.

Somewhere deep inside, the familiarity called to me. In my dreams, like an echo carried on the wind.

I raced to the door and bolted it with trembling hands. Then I pressed my forehead against the solid wood and took deep, steadying breaths.

"I know you're in there." The voice was low and smooth. Cautious, but not unfriendly. I took a deep breath and exhaled slowly. "What do you want?"

I forced the words out even as my defensive magic began to swirl around me. Purple infusions of light glimmered around the dim chamber, and I struggled to retain control.

"It's King Bravadik." Even muffled through the thick wood I could hear the discomfort when he announced himself. The title didn't exactly roll off his tongue.

A reluctant smile tugged at my lips.

What had become of the young man I'd seen in town, all those years ago? What sort of man was he now? How strong? How beautiful? I ached to know, but I had no right. I was the former king's barren widow, and as such, of little use to Bravadik, other than as a reminder of a past he might not want to remember.

"Sire." I swallowed. "How can I be of service?"

"Well," he said, "you could open the door, for a start."

I closed my eyes. *Goddess, if he only knew how much I wanted to.*

"I... I can't." I cast around for an excuse. "I'm undressed, and I am... unwell, Your Majesty."

"I see." An awkward pause ensued. "I have come to ask if you'd join me for dinner at Stavrok and Lucy's castle tonight? They attended my coronation and invited us both."

I couldn't help smiling again at his use of the king and queen's real names. It made sense that Erik wouldn't follow political protocol, given his upbringing. He would be a breath of fresh air in noble circles, and I wished, more than anything, to be there to see him flourish.

But it would break my heart all over again, to be so close to my intended mate and yet be unable to touch him.

I turned and pressed my back against the door. A deep ache was building inside my belly for the man who stood on the other side.

"If you are unwell, however..." His voice fell silent.

"You must go to dinner," I forced myself to say. "Stavrok is everything a king should be. Strong and kind, a true father to his people. And Lucy is a beautiful soul. She's a worthy queen, and a perfect match for him. You could not wish for better mentors, Erik."

There was a heavy silence. Then I realized my mistake.

My eyes squeezed shut. *Damn.*

"Erik? How do you know my name?"

"I..." I swallowed hard and wrapped my arms across my chest. "I saw you once," I said. "Years ago. Magnik pointed you out in the crowd." I cleared my throat at the silence from the other side of the door. "I confess, I kept tabs on you through the years. I hoped one day you would find the way to your rightful position, here at court."

He didn't answer for a long moment. "You're the one who told them where to find me."

I blinked rapidly as tears formed in my eyes. I wanted to hold him so much, kiss away the frown that was surely pulling at his perfect skin. But I had no right.

"I must lie down now, sire. Please, go to dinner. Give them my apologies." My eyes fluttered closed. "Send my blessings to Lucy and the new babies. They will be breathtaking, I know it."

This time I lost the battle, and hot tears slid down my cheeks. To have a baby of my own... it was a long-held dream. A fruitless one, of course, but that didn't stop the need from rising up on occasion.

"I will, Queen Marienne." There was a drawn-out pause from the other side of the door. I pictured him there, waiting. Lingering. "Thank you."

I turned back, and touched my palm to the wood. "I am no longer the queen, Your Majesty. You can call me Marienne. My husband is dead, and you will soon find your own bride who will be queen and rule alongside you."

I heard a soft, light scraping sound against the door, as though he too had pressed his hand against the wood.

"You'll always be a queen, Marienne," he said, and I moved my hand to my mouth to contain the sob that threatened to escape.

Eventually, I sensed him moving away from the door. "Goodnight."

I held my breath as his footsteps retreated down the stone hallway. Once nothing but silence remained, I collapsed onto my bed and began to cry.

My destined lover, my fated mate. He had walked away from me. And my heart broke all over again because I knew it was for the best.

∼

Erik

"What's the fastest way to Stavrok's castle?" I asked Thomas, the head of the house.

I still hadn't quite worked it all out, but he seemed like someone I could trust.

"The fastest, sire?" A smile lit up his face, "Technically, that would be flight."

I grinned. I liked that idea; it would certainly make a statement. Though the lack of clothing on arrival might be a problem.

Thomas smiled even wider, as if he knew where my thoughts had gone. He obviously had a wicked sense of humor and I liked that about him. "Perhaps, since this is your first visit, sire, you could take the carriage?"

I frowned, disappointed. "Flying would be more fun."

Thomas snapped his fingers and several maids arrived holding clothes in their outstretched arms.

"I thought you might say that, so perhaps you would take the carriage today, and take along a few changes of clothes so that next time you wish to visit, you will have something to change into when you arrive."

I slapped him on the back. "You're a genius."

He checked his wristwatch. "And you will soon be late, sire. The carriage has been prepared. It is waiting for you at the castle gates. So please, my king, enjoy your evening and we will see you later tonight. Or tomorrow, if you so choose."

I flicked up my eyebrows. "Tomorrow?"

"Yes. King Stavrok may invite you to stay. If he does, please take the opportunity to view his kingdom in the daylight. There are many changes he has implemented that, if I'm allowed to be frank..."

"Always," I told him.

"That perhaps Your Highness would look at implementing

here. In our clan. For our people." Thomas tilted his head, looking at me thoughtfully. "There is a lot of good you can do, sire."

I nodded. I was under no illusions about being able to rule the kingdom without support from others. This role was new to me, and I welcomed his guidance. "I will certainly take that advice. Thank you, Thomas."

He smiled and indicated the stairs behind me. "You must go. The maids will follow you and pack your clothes for you."

I glanced over at the little blonde woman who was eyeing me as though she would like to do more than lay out my clothes for me. Perhaps she would accompany me for the drive?

"How long is this carriage ride, Thomas?"

Thomas frowned, catching my drift. His eyes flickered over to the maidservant and he dismissed her with a wave of his hand. "Not long enough, sire."

I heaved a sigh and headed toward the stairs. "All right. See you when I see you."

I walked out to the carriage and climbed in, alone, and we set off.

My gut ached, my balls throbbed, and my veins pumped with a fire that was only associated with the need to shift, or fuck.

I needed a woman. It hadn't mattered that a door stood between us; even *speaking* to Marienne had left me hard and wanting. I needed some relief from the pain.

I wasn't sure what it was about that woman. The sound of her voice, so sweet, made my head spin. Even hearing her name spoken, as Lucy had done at the coronation, seemed to set me off.

But she was my half-brother's widow, and a sorceress to boot. She was off-limits.

Yet she stirred my dragon like no other, and I wasn't sure why.

If I ever got my hands on her, I was afraid I may never let her go.

Not that she would want me, I reminded myself, as I always

did whenever my thoughts wandered to Marienne. She'd been wed to my older brother, the king. Surely, compared to him, I was a low-rate, pathetic bastard?

Queen Marienne would never look on me with anything but pity.

THREE

ERIK

Arriving at Stavrok's kingdom was like driving through another dimension. The streets were clean, the houses were all brightly lit and smoke billowed from the chimneys.

His people were obviously wealthy, and it made my stomach churn to think of how my mother and I had lived for so long. The struggle of our friends and neighbors. The taxes on the people. *My* people, now.

When the carriage rolled to a stop outside the actual castle, I got out and stared up at the incredible monument in front of me.

Wow.

The idea that I was invited as a guest to such a place, still felt like a dream.

"This way, sire." A servant took my clothes and walked ahead, up the stairs before me.

I followed him, looking around and absorbing the atmosphere of the place. And once we stepped inside and the warm air hit my face, I sighed.

This was heaven.

There were expensive tapestries on the walls, lush carpets beneath my feet and from the sound of the general chatter and laughter in the castle, happy people around me.

The servant turned toward me. "I believe the main throne room is ahead, sire. I will take these clothes to King Stavrok's staff."

The servant headed off and I stared ahead at the well-lit doorway.

"Erik? Is that you?" Stavrok called from the end of the hallway.

I inhaled deeply and squared my shoulders. Time to be a king. I strode forward, entering the room and realizing it was a large sitting room. A huge fireplace was stoked with wood and welcoming flame, and in front, a set of large leather chairs seemed to beckon. Stavrok stood by with a bottle of alcohol.

I grinned at the huge man and walked forward to greet him. I clasped Stavrok's hand, giving it a firm shake, and smiled in greeting at his wife who stood nearby. "Thank you so much for having me."

"We're excited to have you here!" Lucy said. She had a baby on each broad hip and she juggled them with seeming ease. "But where's Marienne?"

I reached out a hand to the baby boy who grabbed my finger and smiled a toothless, gummy grin at me.

"She was unwell," I said shortly. "She sent her apologies, and told me to come along and learn all I could from you two."

Stavrok chuckled. "Well, she knows best. Come, follow me."

Lucy hoisted the babies on her hips. "I need to put these two back in their cribs. I'll meet you both in the dining room."

She headed off toward the broad staircase at the center of the hall.

I watched her large, swinging hips as she left, then realized I was staring and pulled my gaze back to the king before me. "I apologize. Your family is…"

Everything I could ever want. I couldn't express the thought without sounding odd, but it hung in the air between us.

Stavrok acknowledged my unspoken compliment with a broad, knowing smile. He led me into a huge dining room and poured us both a whiskey. The amber liquid sloshed in the glasses as he picked them up.

"I agree," he said. "I'm a lucky man."

We clinked glasses.

"To a successful alliance between our two great houses," he said.

I nodded. "Hear, hear!"

I took a sip and enjoyed the burn that rolled down my throat. "So, from what I gather, you and my half-brother were not on friendly terms?"

Stavrok let out a booming laugh. "Because I killed him, you mean?"

So, it's true.

I absorbed the information, careful not to let the shock show on my face.

Stavrok had been nothing but friendly to me, but I couldn't let myself forget that this man was powerful as hell. This man had killed the previous ruler of my kingdom.

I simply nodded. Stavrok's smile softened, and he led me over to the dining table. It was huge, and elaborately laid out with crystal glasses, white linen, and sparkling silverware. Seeming to pick up on my uncertainty, he indicated the chair to the left of him. I sat and nodded in gratitude.

He took his place at the head of the table, confident and stately. A true king.

There was a place setting to my left. A wave of sadness passed over me that Marienne would not be here to sit in what I saw as her rightful spot.

"Magnik wanted more than he had," Stavrok said. I put aside

my bleak thoughts about Marienne and refocused. "Always. He craved power, wealth, and domination over the other dragon kingdoms. When he saw a way to force me to hand over my lands, and the mining rights that come with them, he took it."

"What did he do?" I asked.

"He kidnapped Lucy."

My mouth dropped open.

"Excuse me?" I placed my drink on the pristine white tablecloth so that I didn't spill it everywhere. "He... what?"

"He kidnapped me, held me in the dungeon, and threatened to kill me if Stavrok didn't agree to his ransom conditions," Lucy said, as she walked back into the room. Her tone was surprisingly breezy, given the horror of her tale. I wondered if all humans were this nonchalant, or if this one was unusual in that regard.

She sat down on the right side of her husband and laid a hand over his.

"Are our babes sleeping?" he asked her, in a gentle tone that I was surprised to hear from such a strong man.

She nodded, smiling. "Like little angels."

Then she turned her gaze back on me just as I lifted my drink to my lips.

"So... Erik. I assume you have a temper?" She smirked at Stavrok. "It seems to be a feature in the bloodline of dragon kings."

I choked on the whiskey, which shot up my nose and out of my mouth, making a general mess of everything around me.

Servants hurried over from every corner to clean up the spill, handing me napkin after napkin.

"I am sorry," I said, annoyed at myself and embarrassed more than anything.

Could I make it any more obvious that I wasn't raised to be anything other than a street urchin?

Stavrok grinned. "My wife has a wicked tongue. I should be the one apologizing to you."

Lucy glared at him. "I was just asking a question."

Question... question... What had she asked again?

Oh, that was right.

I bowed my head for a moment, gathering my thoughts.

"Well, yes," I answered eventually. "I struggled with my temper a lot when I was younger. Especially through my growth years when I was first shifting. I set the town alight one too many times." I winced. "The people named me Rage.... But my mother called me Erik."

"And you prefer it over your longer name?" Lucy asked.

I inhaled sharply, not sure if I should admit to such a thing. But I didn't wish to answer to Bravadik for the rest of my life, so I spoke honestly. "Yes."

Bravadik, my royal name, still threw me off-balance every time I heard it. My father had told my mother what to call me when I was born, and it had always stuck in my craw that she had allowed him to have such a say over my life as to actually name me.

I never even met the man. He hadn't sent me so much as a letter.

My hosts didn't ask why I preferred the name Erik, however, and the conversation soon turned toward the running of the kingdom. Stravrok was aware that I didn't know the first thing about statecraft, but he didn't seem to hold it against me.

"My father considered the happiness of the people to be the most important part of running a kingdom," Stavrok said. "If the townsfolk are warm, and well fed, then the whole land will prosper. That advice hasn't failed me yet."

I cast my mind back to the hardships I had faced, growing up in a humble village, far away from any finery. The long, dark winters. The famine. The cold nights where my mother had no kindling to keep us warm.

"Everything you told me about King Magnik..." I stared down at my plate. I knew I had to choose my words carefully; kings did not barrel through conversations like these. I had to be smart. "And everything I experienced in the past as one of his subjects... he is not a ruler I wish to emulate."

Lucy snorted.

"But I don't know the kingdom. Not as I should. Not as a *king* would. I..." I wavered. "There has to be a better way of doing things. I vowed to do right by my people when they placed the crown on my head. I want to honor that vow."

Stavrok studied me, as if sizing me up. I looked back, not breaking eye contact. The huge, open fireplace behind us flickered, casting golden light over the table and filling me with a sense of peace I hadn't felt in years.

Lucy opened her mouth as if she was going to say something. But before she could, however, the fireplace roared, flaring with light and heat. Flames shot upward and sparked out of the grate. The room filled with the sound of cutlery clattering against plates as Stavrok, Lucy, and I looked around with astonishment.

"What –" Stavrok began.

At the other end of the room, the double doors opened with a boom. A female figure stood in the doorway, flanked by two servants.

"Your Majesty, Dowager Queen Marienne of the Black Mountains."

I froze in my seat.

Stavrok and Lucy stood up from the table.

"Marienne!" Lucy swept toward the visitor, pleasure visible on her face. "Erik said you were ill! I'm so glad you made it."

Stavrok murmured something to me, but I couldn't understand his words. My head was buzzing. Panic and adrenaline flooded through me, and my heart thundered in my chest.

Marienne stood in the doorway for what felt like an eternity. I watched, transfixed, as she began to move toward us. Everything else in the room grew dimmer as she approached, as though she was giving off her own source of light. Her long dress shimmered and rippled, hugging her gorgeous frame, and her dark hair flowed loosely across her shoulders.

I had never seen anyone more beautiful.

Her eyes captivated me the most. They were a deep indigo, so dark they could have been black. When they caught the light, they glowed with magic and mystery.

My heart clenched at the sight of those eyes.

Something inside me snapped. The barrier that held back my dragon broke, and it thundered to life. My dragon roared, more powerful than ever before, and in that moment, I knew I'd lost all vestiges of control.

I didn't have time to shout a warning. My vision blurred, and the roaring inside my mind grew louder and louder as I slid off my chair, dropped to my knees and succumbed to the inevitable.

The dragon would not be silenced. It had seen Marienne, and in that split second, I was no longer the one calling the shots.

It had been years since I had shifted like this. Wild, spontaneous, and one hundred percent animal instinct. I couldn't do anything but cling on for the ride; already my claws were lengthening, my ribcage expanding. My blurred vision sharpened as the dragon took over, and I let out a roar as my wings unfurled from my back. I beat them through the air, causing the fireplace to flicker and cutlery and glassware to fall to the floor with a clatter and crash.

I twisted around, trying to get my bearings. My human mind screamed out, but it was locked deep within the scaly hide of the dragon.

The dragon was on a mission. It had zeroed in on Marienne. She stood, pale and unmoving, staring up at me with those beautiful eyes.

She was everything I wanted. Everything I needed.

Stavrok inched into my peripheral vision. He had circled around me in a wide arc, careful not to place himself between me and Marienne. Lucy was nowhere to be seen.

He shouted something. With a heroic amount of effort, I wrenched my gaze off the woman in front of me and onto Stavrok.

My claws dragged along the floor as I moved toward him, and I growled, but he didn't back down. He was still yelling.

What was he yelling?

"The windows! Get them open *now*!"

I knew—the part of me that was still a man, anyway—that I didn't want to hurt anyone. But the dragon in me would rip this place apart if anyone tried to stop me from taking Marienne.

The woman herself, in contrast to the chaos around her, stayed remarkably composed. She gazed up at me, like she was waiting for something. I extended my wings out to their full capacity and the rush of air swept her hair back from her face. It fluttered and resettled around her shoulders, and I caught the hint of a smile at the corners of her mouth.

Why was she not afraid of my dragon?

The wind picked up, cold and strong, and my head snapped up. The dragon was more alert than me, and I scanned the room, noting that the row of wide, floor-to-ceiling windows had been thrown open. The curtains billowed out like the sails of a ship, and the star-lit sky glittered beyond.

While I focused on Marienne, Stavrok had shifted, too. His dragon form loomed in the shadows, just as powerful and imposing as the man himself.

A tiny figure pressed up close against his dark, scaly side. *Lucy.*

Stavrok roared. A tongue of flame shot out through his open jaw.

I roared back, then stepped closer to Marienne. I crouched low, inviting her to climb onto my back. She came willingly, sliding over my shoulder and settling between my wings. I shuddered in delight as her tiny hands scrambled for purchase against my scales.

I spared a final glance at Stavrok. Our eyes met, and an understanding passed between us.

Then, I leapt to the closest open window, and launched with Marienne up and into the night.

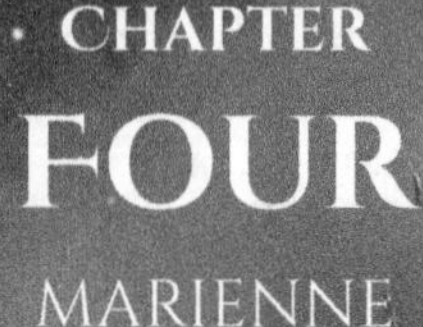

CHAPTER
FOUR

MARIENNE

The harsh winter winds rushed around me, tearing at my hair and gown. If I were fully human, I would have been half-frozen by now.

But I wasn't just a woman. My magic shimmered and pulsed through the air, sending trails of heat through my core. Erik's huge shoulders shifted beneath me, and I moaned at the wonderful sensation of touching him. Could he feel my warmth spreading through his back as he flew? My legs clenched tight around him, and his wings beat the air with renewed force.

Power simmered in my veins. In that moment, I could have moved mountains if I had to. I needed Erik, and I was hopeful that nothing would stand in our way tonight.

I was so caught up in my musings I barely registered when his feet hit the stony parapet of the high North Tower. I let out a breathless laugh when his wings brushed against my back, preventing me from falling off during the abrupt landing.

Such a gentleman.

He released me, and I slid off his back, moving away so he had space to shift back to human when he was ready.

He staggered back from me. The air was already shimmering, and before my eyes the dragon dissolved away, leaving the man, naked and panting, in its place.

This moment—here and now—felt like our first true meeting.

There wasn't anything between us any longer. No husband, no ceremony, no court protocol to follow. We were completely alone.

Erik was tall and lean, with shaggy hair that fell to his sharp jawline. His stature was powerful; anyone could see at a glance that he was a true dragon king.

He was trembling. His eyes were shadowed, and his face turned away. He wouldn't look at me.

Was he afraid?

Had he felt my magic as we were flying back to the castle? A shockwave of pain seared through my chest at the possibility of his rejection. Did he think I would hurt him?

I reached out a hand toward him, and he flinched.

"Don't," he said, his voice low and gravelly. The words shot right to my core, and warmth spread through my belly, even as a sob caught in my throat.

He didn't want my touch.

Slowly, I retracted my hand. We stood on the castle rooftop, at a stalemate. Neither of us moved. I was pretty sure neither of us breathed.

Then, his gaze slid to meet mine, just for a second, before darting away.

Oh.

He wasn't trembling out of fear. He was holding himself *back*.

I could see it now, the tightness in his strong frame. The way the muscles bunched together in his forearms as he squeezed his hands into white-knuckled fists.

It had been five long years since anyone had touched me.

The day I'd seen Erik, everything changed. From the moment I realized he was my fated mate, I knew I could never give myself to the king again. Magnik declared me barren when I said, 'no more', and he lost interest in me completely in a sexual way.

I hadn't been able to give Magnik heirs, but I could give him the power he sought. He valued the latter far more than anything else. He agreed to the physical separation happily enough. Our marriage bed had been cold ever since.

With Magnik, there had been no intimacy and, for years, I had convinced myself I didn't need such things in my life.

But I was wrong. So wrong. And standing here in front of Erik, the longing for him drowned me, flooding my senses until I couldn't think about anything else.

I *needed* him.

Slowly, so as not to startle him, I crept forward. My steps were feather-light against the flagstones—I could move soundlessly when I wanted to—and I kept my stance loose and relaxed.

I wasn't afraid.

He wouldn't hurt me.

We were so close now that I could feel the body heat coming off him in waves. It warmed the air around us and intensified my own desire. Gently, I reached out and cupped his forearm, encouraging it toward my body. His trembling increased. I placed his large, hot hand against my skin, over the neck of my low-cut gown.

My chest heaved beneath his touch, and ripples of warmth spread through me, undercutting the coldness of the night. The ripples became waves, lapping into every corner of my mind and body. Like a prism, the world exploded with light and color.

The images came to me in flashes. A silk canopy. A cheering crowd, flower petals thrown into a blue sky. Vows, an altar. Laughter, wine glasses sparkling in the sunlight. My hands trailing over his bare chest. His arms encircling me, protecting me. A kingdom—*our* kingdom—bright and thriving. Life renewing, fruit trees blossoming. Our children, running alongside us as we walked together, unhurried. Free, happy, fulfilled.

The visions vanished as quickly as they had come, slipping away into the darkness. All that remained was Erik.

His eyes flashed, and his hand flexed against me. I wanted to close the remaining distance between us, but I waited, mouth parted. If his hand slid down an inch, he would feel how hard my nipples had become.

His mouth crashed against mine without warning. I groaned at the feel of him as his other hand encircled my waist, drawing me up into him until I was on tiptoes and pressed against his hardness.

He pushed his tongue against mine and my legs trembled. No-one had ever held me like this—with such blatant raw need.

He kissed me with single-minded intensity, hands roaming all over my body until I gave up trying to kiss him back and simply clung onto his huge arms.

He gathered up my skirts, his hands spanned over my thighs, desperate, rough, and unrelenting.

I arched against him, impatient. I wanted him. So badly it *hurt.*

He pulled me up into his arms, fluid and decisive. I pressed my face into his shoulder, trailing my mouth over the hot skin of his neck, the angle of his jaw.

He was carrying me somewhere.

Inside?

I didn't care. I felt the wave of warmth settle across my skin, felt the motion of his long strides, but I couldn't bring myself to look up, or even open my eyes. If there was anyone around to see us, I preferred not to know.

We passed through a door, then another. The world spun around as he shifted me in his arms before dropping me onto a soft, warm, surface.

Is this a bed? How thoughtful of him.

I didn't have time to think beyond that, as he crawled up over me and lowered the entire length of his body down onto mine.

If he had been holding back before, he wasn't now. I groaned, pinned between him and the mattress. His hot breath huffed in my ear, and when he shifted on me, the hard length of his cock pressed against my stomach.

I rolled my hips up to meet his. He withdrew a little and loomed over me on all fours. He truly was beautiful, especially like this, his eyes slightly unfocused and swimming with lust.

"Erik..." I whispered.

"You want this? As much as I do?"

"Yes..."

He closed his hand around the neckline of my gown; the sheer, gauzy material crumpled in his fist. I moaned as he tugged sharply and tore the fabric in half, exposing my aroused breasts and belly to the air. His groan was deep and lustful, before his hot, damp mouth closed over one of my nipples, and I bit my lip to hold in the cry of pleasure that threatened to release.

He growled against my skin and palmed my other breast. I slid the remains of my gown off my shoulders to give him better access, writhing beneath him until the teasing became too much for both of us.

He reared back, ripping and tugging until the rest of my clothing was gone from the bed, then his mouth returned to my breasts where he laved first one, then the other, of my sensitized flesh with an expertise I reveled in.

"I need more," I whispered, and dragged his mouth up to meet mine. As he kissed me, deeply, I felt his essence tangle with mine and permeate the air around us. I pulled him down on me, encouraging the contact. My pussy was soaked, and I only grew more desperate when I finally felt every inch of his firm, naked body against mine.

We rocked together, rejoicing in the feeling. I groaned when his hand twisted into my hair and pulled my head back, exposing my neck under his mouth. He laved kisses over my throat, his tongue darting out to taste my skin. I moved again and my center dragged up over the length of his cock. We both shivered at the sensation, and his hands slid lower, bracketing my hips.

He panted hard. Every inhalation and exhalation shot through his body, like he'd been running for miles. I wasn't in a much better state myself.

Slowly, agonizingly slowly, he lifted me up by the hips and put me into position.

Then he sank into me, inch by inch. We both cried out at the connection. I was so tight, and his thickness felt so unbelievably good I had to take a moment to steady myself. My pussy rippled slowly around him, and I whimpered as I wrapped my legs around his waist, embracing the feeling of fullness.

I could have stayed that way forever. His ragged breaths were hot against my cheek. I bit at the corner of his mouth, and he grunted, thrusting up into me.

And again. And again. He fucked me hard and fast and… perfectly. The intensity of my pleasure shocked me. Sweetness rose like a cresting wave, and when his rough hand worked its way between us, fingers circling around my clit, I couldn't hold back a scream as a violent orgasm crashed over me.

I shuddered against him, working my hips up and down, urging him deeper with every thrust. Our mouths found each other, tasting, elevating the intensity of the experience.

His cock drove into me relentlessly, and he buried his face into my neck as he came. When I felt him pulse inside me, I gave myself over to the sensation completely. I panted his name over and over as I came again. I couldn't do anything but cling to him mindlessly as we kissed and shuddered in a mutual, mind-blowing climax.

He was still buried inside me, and nothing else mattered but the two of us, in this bed. Darkness filled the night, but here in his arms, I was completely safe.

The last thing I registered was Erik pressing a soft kiss against my temple, and then sleep pulled me under.

I don't know how long I lay there in the darkness, holding Marienne in my arms.

Even though I was exhausted, every muscle in my body wrung out and sated, my mind buzzed. In sleep, Marienne burrowed into my chest, and my heart melted. I brushed her long, dark hair off her bare shoulder and smiled to myself as I tucked her closer against me.

I couldn't make sense of what had just happened.

My shifter was a powerful one; my royal bloodline made sure of that. I had always been stronger than the other men in my village, and my dragon could fly great distances without tiring.

Sure, I had a reputation for losing my temper. But uncontrollable shifting, and then claiming my half-brother's wife? That was on a different level. In truth, the lack of control scared me.

There seemed to be one common denominator. One factor that set my dragon off like no other.

And I was currently sharing a bed with her.

If I hadn't just experienced the most mind-blowing sex of my life, I might have been more concerned. As it was, I couldn't bring myself to worry too much. The evening had taken an unexpected turn, but not an unwelcome one.

I should probably send Stavrok and Lucy a thank you gift basket.

I almost laughed aloud at the thought, but managed to keep in the sound, fearful I would wake my lover. I ran a hand over Marienne's soft hair and drifted into sleep.

Marienne

My eyes, still blurry with sleep, took a couple of seconds to adjust when I opened them.

Unless I was mistaken, I was in King Erik's bedchamber.

Huh.

The room was large and beautiful, and through an archway I spied a small sitting area with a vista through the window that overlooked the snowy mountains. The silk canopy over the bed exactly matched the one I had seen in my vision.

These rooms at the top of the North Tower had stood empty for years. Magnik and I had never slept here. He preferred to sleep nearer the heart of the castle, where the bank vaults lay filled with gold coins and other treasures.

My old rooms in the East Tower had been at the other end of the castle from Magnik. As far away from him as possible.

Erik didn't know about any of that.

To him, these rooms likely meant nothing. They were simply the king's rooms, prepared for him as befitted the man who currently sat upon the throne. The servants had removed dust sheets, polished the candelabra, and swept back the curtains to reveal the rolling hills of the valley below us. Glowing coals slumbered in the grate, and the bearskin rug spread out before the fire looked soft and inviting.

On a whim, I slipped out from between the sheets and padded

over to sink my bare feet into the rug. I had always thought of this castle as gloomy and oppressive, but with Erik by my side, I was starting to appreciate its beauty.

A grumble came from the bed. Erik had flung out an arm into the empty space. His face was buried in the pillow, but I could already picture his furrowed, displeased brow. He was no good at hiding his emotions, even in sleep.

With a smile, I crept back to bed. He enveloped me with his long limbs, and I sighed with contentment and relaxed against him, readily submitting to the cuddling.

The king's bed in the royal suite. I never thought I'd actually end up here.

It was ironic, given I had been Magnik's wife, but somehow, I felt more like a queen right now, than ever before.

I fell asleep again wrapped in Erik's arms, with a smile lifting my lips.

When I woke, warm, golden sunlight poured into the bedchamber.

I was no longer within the tangle of his limbs. I lay curled up on my own side of the bed. I could feel the indentation of his weight behind me, but we must have separated at some point.

I suppressed my disappointment and rolled over to face him.

He was already awake. His gaze slid away from mine, his expression guilty, like I'd caught him out on something.

Had he been watching me sleep? My lips quirked into a smile.

After a minute, he grinned back. There was a hint of hesitation, but his expression was warm and genuine all the same.

"Marienne..." His eyes roved over my face, dipping lower before snapping up again. I suppressed a giggle. He had seen much more than my bare shoulders after all. "Last night... I must apologize."

I tilted my head, confused. I wanted nothing more than to curl into him once more, run my hands over his chest and press my mouth against his. But I resisted.

"I wasn't aware there was anything to apologize for," I said, keeping my tone gentle.

Unless...

The room was still toasty warm, but a shiver ran up my spine. "Did you not wish to have me, sire?"

"No!"

My mouth dropped open, and I met his gaze with wide eyes. *He didn't want me?* "I...err..." I didn't know what to say, but he shook his head.

"I mean... *yes.* I did, Marienne. I..." He swallowed. "I *do.*"

Relief and pleasure thrummed through me. "Then, sire—"

"Please," he interrupted. "Don't call me that."

"You're my king," I said carefully. "I will do as you wish, of course."

Somehow, he looked even more miserable. My heart sank. I wanted him, and he *clearly* wanted me.

So why did the space between us in this bed feel as though a chasm lay between us?

"Marienne... I just meant, call me Erik. Please." He reached out to lay a hand over mine. The touch was sweet and simple. A mile away from everything that had occurred last night.

I stared down at the bedsheets. His fingers over mine were light, as though he was afraid I might throw him off any second. He had big hands, and my smooth, pale fingers fluttered under his roughened palm.

Then the visions came.

It happened without warning. Usually, I got a couple of seconds to prepare before a premonition took over, but this one hit me like a sledgehammer, pulling me under, drowning me in its intensity.

I gasped before reality ripped away from me and I was flung out into the darkness.

The world reformed; solidified. I found myself outside, on my knees, looking up at the castle. The sky overhead was black, but the castle was brighter than I had ever seen. Every turret, every window, *everything* burned. Hot tongues of flame shot into the sky, lighting up the night, and thick clouds of acrid smoke filled the air. I choked, coughing. I couldn't speak. My throat was raw from screaming. All I knew was heat and destruction.

The castle melted away. I was in a busy street. A town marketplace. I recognized it with a jolt; this was the village where I first saw Erik.

That day had been bright. The sky was blue, the trees laden with apple blossom, and the crowds cheered for their new young queen. *Me.*

This time, however, the sky thundered overhead. People ran, screaming, past me. I skittered backwards but they didn't notice. I was a ghost, powerless to help them, or to stop it. Death hung in the air.

It was then that I realized the flashes in the sky weren't lightning, but dragon fire.

The image changed again. I was back in the castle, on the rooftop. I knelt, cradling a man in my arms.

Erik gazed up at me. Despite the blood and dirt that covered his face, he looked peaceful. Serene, even.

A smattering of raindrops fell against his cheek. It took me a second to realize that they weren't raindrops. They were tears. Mine.

He reached up and touched my cheek. The motion clearly hurt him, and with horror I saw the wound in his chest. Beyond healing, even with magic.

"Erik..." I whispered, stricken.

He just smiled. His face was close to mine, and I bent so I could catch his soft words.

"Our baby," he breathed. "Get as far away from here as you can."

My breath hitched on a sob, and the vision melted away. I tumbled through darkness for what felt like forever, until I registered arms around me. Strong, solid and real.

"Marienne!" Erik—whole, uninjured, and frowning deeply—cradled my face, wiping away the tears that tracked down my cheeks with his thumbs. "Marienne. What is it? What's wrong?"

I gasped, trying to get a hold of myself. I ran my hands up and down his arms, feeling his warm skin beneath my palms to reassure myself he was there. That he was alive.

All the distance between us was gone. We were tangled together again in the bedsheets like one body; one being.

I pressed my forehead against his, allowing myself a couple of heartbeats to recover from the vision. I breathed Erik in, feeling him against me, warm and solid. He was safe. Unharmed. He held me against him. It felt so good.

I couldn't afford to become distracted. Something bad was coming this way and I needed time to gather my thoughts and work out what the visions had meant.

Reluctantly, I slid off the bed in search of some clothes. The ones I'd worn last night weren't in a state to be worn again. There wasn't anything in the walk-in wardrobe except large robes, so I slid one around my shoulders and tied the strap around the middle. It was awkward, but better than leaving this room naked.

When I reappeared in the main room, Erik lay exactly where I had left him in the middle of the bed. He looked like a lost puppy.

I walked toward the door.

"Wait."

I froze, one hand on the doorhandle. When I turned, his gaze was steady. I looked away, cheeks burning with the knowledge that he had just witnessed me in such a state.

"Tell me." Even from his position on the bed, he still commanded my attention. "Are you okay, Marienne?"

I managed to nod. In the face of everything I'd just seen, his concern warmed me straight to the core.

"Yes." I bit my lip. I wanted to explain myself, but I needed to make sense of it all first. "See you later?"

I stepped out of the room before he could reply.

SIX

ERIK

I'd been called into a meeting with the elders, and I was so out of my depth I could barely breathe.

Important matters were being discussed. Matters of state, matters that I had to attend to now, as the king.

I couldn't concentrate on any of it for a single, *stupid* reason.

I felt underdressed in my own damned Council meeting.

I eyed the thick gold chain that hung around the neck of Elder Kilgrave. It glinted as he turned, winking at me as if to say, *look at all this finery. Where's yours, boy?*

That chain could have fed my mother and me for a year. Longer, probably. The elder caught my eye, raising his brow, and I flushed, glaring down at the table.

It wasn't that I wanted a similar decoration for myself. I couldn't imagine anything worse than parading around in such a wasteful thing, in fact.

But maybe that was because I was too roughshod, too unsophisticated. A mere boy, playing at being a king.

"Sire?"

My head snapped up at the address. The other advisor, Elder Slater, pressed his lips into a thin, disapproving line as he stared at me.

He wasn't much friendlier than his counterpart. Every time I had to ask for clarification on a point of business, he gave an impatient *tut*, like I hadn't been paying attention or was too stupid to understand matters of grave importance.

I wanted to call an end to the whole meeting, and fly out to find a grassy field where I could spend the time roaming around and exploring the countryside like I used to do. Maybe I could take Marienne with me. The image of her laid out naked in a field somewhere filled my mind, and I grinned to myself.

Maybe we could go for round two...

I coughed loudly, forcing myself back into the present. "Sorry, what was the question?"

"We need to decide how to allocate our spending for the next quarter, sire. The old king raised taxes on the townsfolk last year, and now we have..." The elder paused, a smirk sliding over his face. "We have something of a surplus, it seems."

"That's excellent news." I spread out my hands. "I've been doing some thinking on that subject myself."

"Is that so?" Elder Slater interjected. He added, "Your Majesty," when I turned toward him and speared him with a look.

Somehow, the way he said it made the phrase sound like a question, rather than the statement of fact it was.

"Yes." I straightened up. I refused to be cowed by either of these men. I was now their king, whether they—or I—liked it or not. I knew my own instincts well enough, and they'd rarely let me down before. What I was about to say, felt right. "I want to issue a decree," I announced. "Our people shall have free heating, and water, and electricity. All of the costs will be covered by the Crown."

"But sire—"

I held up a hand, interrupting Elder Slater. "You won't change my mind. I've spoken to Stavrok about this," I continued, ignoring the matching glowers I received from both of the elders. "I don't see why the system that works so well for his kingdom can't also work for ours."

Elder Kilgrave clutched a hand over his heavy chain, like I was about to rip it off his neck at any moment and hand it over to the poor. "Your Majesty. Those funds are needed for castle upkeep." He pursed his mouth. "Not the trivial plight of the common folk."

I refrained from pointing out that, until very recently, *I* had been one of the common folk of whom he spoke with such disdain.

A single, pointed glance around the high-ceilinged chamber told me the whole story. The grand fireplace. The gilt mirrors. The sparkling gilded ceiling. This was where the money was spent. On excessive luxuries that were not necessary, nor had any function.

Perhaps I should consider taking that necklace of his and using it to feed the hungry.

"I can't see any urgent repairs that need doing." I tilted my head and narrowed my eyes, daring them to disagree. "Please, feel free to point out anything I might have missed."

"What Elder Kilgrave *means*, sire," Elder Slater began, rolling up the documents spread out over the table in front of us, "is that the royal funds are a serious matter. Frivolous spending such as this... it would not be a good start to your reign. Please trust that we are trying to *help* you."

The way he said it left no room for debate. He spoke as though I were an ignorant child who needed to be taught a lesson, instead of a full-grown man. Their leader.

I clenched my jaw, tight. The room, so cozy and elegant only moments before, felt stuffy and restrictive. The walls pressed in on me and a wave of crushing claustrophobia sent me reeling.

It wasn't in my nature to back away from a fight. But I couldn't let my temper rise. Now that I was king, I needed to wield far more control over my emotions than I ever had before.

This was a battle I didn't know how to win. This wasn't some bar fight; this was politics. I didn't have the right weapons, and the rulebook was a total mystery to me.

I was forced to retreat. My heart pounding, I yanked open the door and left the council chamber before they could patronize me further. And before my rage could fully ignite.

I was totally out of my depth. I may have forestalled my temper for today, but what about tomorrow? Or the next day? Or next week?

What did I know about statecraft? Or leadership? I was playing pretend, a dragon king in name only.

It was merely a matter of time before everyone in the whole kingdom would come to realize it.

~

Marienne

I SPENT the better part of the morning walking around my suite in the East Tower out of sheer force of habit.

I knew every nook and cranny, every pile of books, every cushion and candle. This was my domain, my sanctuary. Nobody was allowed inside without my express permission.

When Magnik had been alive, I wasn't queen of much. But this space, right here in the tower... this was my tiny little kingdom. My small tower room where I worked my magic, far away from the prying eyes of the court.

Now, I knew what I needed to do.

I steeled my nerves and set about pulling various herbs off the shelves and rifling through my library until I found the small, leather-bound volume I sought, right at the top of one of my bookshelves.

In silver letters, the title read: *Psychic Projection.*

I carried the book over to my desk, laid it carefully next to the small bowl I used for spell work, and leafed through the pages.

Projection was not a field of magic in which I had much experience. There were other sorcerers in the realm who specialized in the art of traveling to far-off places in their mind's eye, all while remaining physically safe inside their own territory.

Magnik had tried to force me to learn the art on more than one occasion, so I could spy on neighboring kingdoms for him, but I had never mastered it.

Now that he was dead, I could admit the truth to myself: I'd never really *wanted* to master it. Not for him.

I'd always wanted to *help* people with my magic, not spy on them.

However, this was different.

This time, it felt like I had no choice.

I *had* to know. I needed to find the source of the horrifying images that flashed to the forefront of my mind every time I closed my eyes.

The visions had splintered my happiness into tiny shards. I couldn't wait any longer. There was too much at stake to sit passively and wait for my kingdom to fall into ruin.

I murmured an incantation and a small ball of blue flame hovered over the palm of my hand. Slowly, I lowered it into the bowl and set fire to the bundle of herbs.

A thick, blue smoke rose from the bowl. I forced myself to lean in closer, breathing in the bitter fumes and trying not to cough.

This was the tricky part.

I had to clear my mind totally and *focus.* It was normally a challenge to shut my brain down and induce the visions, but this time, they were all I could think about.

My vision began to swirl. The world dissolved, melting away into blackness.

I concentrated on what I had seen before. The castle burning. People screaming. I flinched but forced myself to look deeper, beyond the pain and suffering.

I need to find the source...

In a flash, the world turned white.

I gasped in shock as phantom snow drifted against my face, settling on my cheeks and eyelashes. Cold air raked my skin, and I whirled, trying to get my bearings in the frozen iceland.

A castle loomed through the blizzard, with towering turrets and a heavy iron drawbridge, built to withstand a thousand winters.

Shock sent me reeling as I perceived the truth.

Damon.

The loner king. The Dragon of Winter.

He had many names. In truth, I knew more of those than I had memories of seeing him in person. He rarely ventured south. He preferred to stay in his icy domain, and usually stayed out of the politics and petty rivalries of the other kingdoms.

His people occasionally traveled south to trade. They were a distinctive sight, wearing thick, heavy furs draped across their shoulders, adding bulk and wildness to their broad, solid frames. Their rough-hewn weapons always looked as if they had seen their fair share of use.

Even Damon's shifters were unique. The northern dragons were pale shades of gray and white. They blended perfectly with their landscape, flying unseen through ice storms and nesting on snowy mountaintops. The fire they breathed was different: not orange, but a luminous, icy blue.

As I stared up at those spiky, foreboding towers, a chill of dread settled in the pit of my stomach.

In that moment, I knew I didn't need to look any further. The threat would come from the north.

SEVEN

ERIK

I managed to release my anger about my doomed meeting with the elders by pacing up and down the corridor outside the council room, practically wearing a hole in the stones underfoot.

After that, I wandered aimlessly through the castle hallways. Soon enough, I ended up totally disorientated.

It began to dawn on me all over again—I didn't know this place. I hadn't yet had a chance to become familiar with the layout. I had no bolt holes, no secret corners, nowhere I could go to lick my wounds.

This was my domain—my literal castle—and I was lost.

All the servants I passed along the way inclined their heads with deference, but from the sideways looks on their faces it was clear they saw me for what I was. A total stranger.

Worthy of respect, sure. I was their king, now. But they didn't know me, and I didn't know them. Perhaps they hated me? How could I live up to the legacy of my half-brother, even if he had been disliked for actions such as kidnapping Stavrok's mate? At least he'd been a true-born king. I was, at best, an interloper.

Eventually I found my way back to a section of the castle I recognized.

In the end, I returned to my office in the council chambers, out of a lack of a better idea on where to go.

The space was empty. The elders presumably gave up the meeting as a lost cause. It was just as well. A headache was building behind my eyes, and I wanted nothing more than a stiff drink and a fuck—in whichever order they came to me.

That was where Marienne found me half an hour later, with my head resting on my arms as I sat at my desk, surrounded by dozens of law codes, balance sheets, and tax bills.

I must have been a pathetic sight.

There was a tentative touch on my shoulder and I knew instantly it was her. I tried not to sink into her touch, though her hand was as light as a feather, and strangely comforting.

When I lifted my head, there was nothing of the fiery temptress who had shared my bed last night. In the mid-morning light, she was wan and frail, flitting around the side of the desk like a butterfly and settling into the unoccupied chair.

She truly is like no woman I've ever met.

And yet, there was something off about her today. She wasn't meeting my eyes.

Something had happened earlier, while we were in bed. Something that had shaken her to the core.

She had rushed off without explaining and instinct had told me not to stop her, but I sensed I was about to find out what had occurred.

"To what do I owe the pleasure?" I kept my voice light, trying not to show any hint of the anxiety that stirred within me.

"I..." She lay her hands, palm-side down, on the desk top and finally met my gaze. "I owe you an apology," she said.

My chin snapped up. Something churned in the pit of my stomach.

Does she regret what happened between us?

I raised an eyebrow. "For what?"

"For rushing off like that... after..." She bit her lip, looking embarrassed. I forced myself not to stare at the way she caught her full lower lip between her teeth.

"Oh." It was my turn to feel uncomfortable. "There's no need to apologize, Marienne. You were under no obligation to stay."

She seemed disappointed to hear that. My confusion grew by the second.

"Wait, is that why you're here?" I asked. "Simply to apologize?"

She sighed. "No. Not entirely."

I could sense that she was stalling, but I couldn't guess why. I raised my eyebrows, waiting.

"You know that I have magic." The words rushed out of her so fast I almost didn't catch them.

"Of course."

She flushed, tucking a long strand of hair behind her ear. "So, I'm a sorceress. That's why Magnik chose me to become his queen. Because he wanted access to my magic. For himself."

At the mention of the previous king, my stomach sank. "Why do you ask?"

"Sometimes I..." She swallowed. "Sometimes I have visions. And when we were together this morning..." Her eyes darted away again. "I saw something, Erik. A vision. That's why I... That's what happened. I had a vision, and I ran."

I exhaled, relief washing over me. She hadn't run because she regretted our coupling. I thought back to the moment she'd left. In truth, she'd looked scared and vulnerable. Like she was a thousand miles away, not safe with me, in our bed.

"Does it hurt?" I asked.

Marienne seemed thrown by the question. "What?"

"When you have your visions."

A strange look crossed her face. "No-one's ever asked me that before. I suppose I'm used to them. I've always had visions, ever since I can remember."

"That doesn't answer my question." My voice was gentle, but I couldn't hide my curiosity.

"It's not a physical pain," she said. "But it's like the world around me disappears. Sometimes I can't trust that what I'm seeing is really... real."

On impulse, I reached out across the desk and clasped her hand.

"There," I said simply. "That's real."

Her face softened, and her thumb stroked across the back of my hand. "It is indeed." She contemplated our joined hands for a moment, then raised her beautiful eyes to mine. "But Erik, I must tell you what I saw." Her expression was grave. She grew even paler than when she'd first entered the room. "I came to warn you."

I frowned. "Of what?"

"Something's coming. A darkness." She broke off, her eyes wide and distressed. "King Damon is planning to attack. I saw the castle burn. Our people, dead in the streets. I—I watched you die in my arms, Erik."

A tear fell down her cheek, glinting silver in the sunlight.

I stared at the open book in front of me without really seeing it. *She saw me die?*

My gaze drifted to our joined hands.

"In your vision. We were... together?"

Warmth bloomed in my chest when I said the words out loud. They felt right. Marienne and me. *Together.*

Her gaze slid away from me. Gently, she disentangled her fingers from mine and withdrew, leaving me oddly bereft.

"Yes." Those lovely eyes refused to meet mine.

My surprise hung in the air between us.

"Surely you've already noticed?" she said. "You must feel it."

My heart hammered in my chest. She sounded resigned; regretful.

"Noticed *what*?" I tried to hold back the harsh tone, but I was getting frustrated. "Feel what?"

"Our connection." Finally, she looked up.

"Of course, I have."

My heart rate increased when I stared as if hypnotized into her eyes. They swirled and shimmered like depthless pools. "The bond between us. The moment we laid eyes on one another, everything changed." She bit her lip, and I suppressed a sigh of longing. "Your dragon knows me, doesn't it? Why do you think it stirs every time you see me? Every time you hear my name. We were meant for each other, Erik. We are soul mates."

Soul mates? Fated to be together?

It was like a final puzzle piece falling into place.

That was why she had hidden from me when I first came to the castle. All these years, she must have known. And I hadn't had a clue.

Something had drawn us toward each other, binding us together. Like a thread running through our lives, winding us closer and closer. Right from the moment we'd seen each other, all those years ago.

My mind was blank with shock. *Soul mates. Fated mates.*

"You knew about this?" I whispered. "The whole time? Why didn't you say anything earlier?"

She looked utterly miserable. My chest tightened as realization struck.

She doesn't want this. Us.

Why would she? Marienne was powerful, beautiful and strong in her own right. Anyone who laid eyes on her could see that she was in a different league to me.

Apparently, the fates had shackled her to me, a low-born lout who was only here by sheer dumb luck.

"It's complicated," she said. "Last night..."

My skin prickled as I remembered the way I had held her in my arms. The passion, the lust, the inescapable desire. It was all due to the fated mate bond?

My chair scraped back from the desk as I stood. My movements were abrupt and jerky; it took a second for me to realize I was shaking with anger.

"You don't have to explain yourself to me," I said, turning away. "I understand now." She didn't want me, but had no choice except to follow fate's design.

The magic had forced her into it. Was that the problem?

I didn't want to see the disgust in her expression. Or, worse, the pity.

"It wasn't my choice, Erik." Her voice was closer now, and when I turned my head, she stood right in front of me. "Neither of us have a choice in this. I'm sorry."

Her eyes flashed with repressed emotion.

I ached to pull her against me with every fiber of my being, but I resisted. I couldn't bear to face her inevitable rejection.

Our bond was inescapable, inevitable. I was still reeling from the truth, but I couldn't deny it: we *were* bonded. Worst of all, some part of me had already known, ever since that first day, when we were worlds apart. When she hung on the arm of King Magnik, her husband, radiant in the sunlight, waving out at the cheering crowds.

I closed my eyes.

"It seems that the fates have a sick sense of humor," I said. "Shackling you to your husband's low-born half-brother. You wanted the king, and you got the bastard."

As soon as I uttered the words, I regretted them. I knew I was being unfair; Marienne had already told me Magnik had chosen *her*, not the other way around. How could anyone say no to a king?

But pain made me harsh. The barbs that had twisted themselves into my heart tightened as her eyes filled with tears.

"Since you arrived in the castle, I wondered about you. Who you were, what kind of man you have become, since that day I saw you in the street." Her strong tone belied the tears that spilled over, tracking down her flushed cheeks. "I think I finally have my answer."

"I guess you do," I snarled. "I am truly sorry to disappoint you, Your Majesty."

I made sure to imbue the title with the same disdain I had received from the elders this morning. Her eyes widened, and then narrowed.

"So am I," she said. "Your *Majesty*."

We breathed in tandem, inches apart. I fought back the desire that pumped through my veins, the warmth I could feel radiating between us.

It didn't matter what our bodies wanted for us. I would never be good enough for her, and we both knew it.

At least we were on the same page. My status in life might have changed, but one thing was certain: last night had been a huge mistake.

She had just made that abundantly clear.

I wasn't worthy of touching her. And I never would be.

· CHAPTER ·

EIGHT

MARIENNE

I stared up at Erik.

His tall, lean body was stiff with tension, and his arms were crossed over his chest. His whole frame, which had been such a comforting haven to me only a few short hours ago, was now as impenetrable as a brick wall.

Hopelessness threatened to crush me. I scrubbed the tears off my cheeks and whirled around, determined to put some distance between the two of us.

I took a few deep breaths to stop the panic from rising up and choking me.

If my fated mate truly didn't want me...

Without Erik, my life would be pure loneliness.

My magic simmered in my veins, an ever-present reminder of the reason why I would always be an outcast. It was the one thing that truly set me apart from others. I'd spent my life gifted and cursed in equal measure.

I knew all the stories. Terrible things happened to sorcerers who were rejected by their mates because their magic could never be accepted. When I was a child, the villagers had whispered tales of madness and destruction wrought by those wielding magic when they had been abandoned by the ones who should have loved them.

I heard of sorceresses who flung themselves off high towers out of despair, or leveled entire towns with their magic. At best, if Erik fully rejected me, I could end up powerless. At worst, I could die.

Still, he had every reason to be upset.

I was hardly a desirable choice. Men had always lusted after my magic, but they feared it, too.

Whatever kindness Erik had shown me, it was clear he was no exception. He didn't see me as a woman, a true partner. He just saw a powerful sorceress who could pose a threat to his reign.

To add insult to injury, I had been Magnik's queen for years without ever conceiving a child. The castle physicians had all concluded I was barren.

Tears pricked my eyes. It was almost too much to bear.

But I couldn't let his rejection overwhelm me. I had to focus. Erik, and his kingdom, needed help.

I steadied myself and turned around. Erik was watching me with an unreadable expression. I forced my features to remain neutral in the face of his indifference. Internally, my heart was close to breaking.

"King Damon." I circled the table, drawing closer to Erik. "There's no time to waste."

It didn't matter how he felt about me right now. I could tell he was still angry, but we had to put aside our differences. We were still allies, first and foremost.

I might not be the queen any longer, but this kingdom is mine as well as his.

He gave a short nod. "How much time do we have?"

I shrugged. "I'm afraid the visions aren't precise. But..." I bit my lip, thinking hard. "It was snowing pretty heavily, which means it will still be winter when they attack."

"Very soon, then." He furrowed his brow as he leaned over the desk, sweeping papers and books aside. "The northern territories are three days' journey from here, correct?"

I adjusted to the swift change of tone in our conversation. He was addressing me in short, clipped phrases, like I was a member of his council.

Very well. I could keep this meeting professional. Maybe he would even let me stay in the castle, in my suite. *Could I learn to live like that, knowing my fated mate was so close by?*

Sooner or later, he would take a wife. And on that day, my heart would *truly* break.

I inclined my head. "By carriage ride, yes." I looked away, shamefaced. "It would be much faster to fly, but... I have no shifting ability, sire."

"Really?" he asked, his eyebrows lifting high on his forehead.

"It's the price of my magic." I shrugged. "You can't miss something you never had."

He opened his mouth, then closed it again.

"I could carry you," he said. "As long as we keep you warm enough."

I shook my head again. "Damon's mountains are dangerously cold. I'm not sure I would survive a long flight in that weather." *Even with my magic to keep me warm.* "Plus, it may be smarter to move with stealth. We would not be inconspicuous if we arrived by flight. Your dragon would be too obvious."

Erik nodded slowly, as though thinking over my words.

"I will lead an expedition to the northern territories." He stood upright, his jaw set and his eyes firm. "We'll gather what intel we can, and then go from there."

A flush of warmth rose in my chest as I looked at him. This man was a natural-born leader. He would make a wonderful king.

"Okay." I lifted my chin, meeting his gaze with more confidence than I felt. "When do we leave?"

Confusion filled his expression. "What?"

I tilted my head. "Sooner rather than later, I should think. Today, or tomorrow?"

"Marienne…" He shook his head at me. A frown fell over his face. "You can't really want to come with me, surely? It's too dangerous."

I bristled. "Excuse me?"

He swept a hand over his face, his features wrinkling as if with stress.

"It's the far north, Marienne! We don't know what we're up against yet, what kind of danger could be waiting for us. I'm not putting you—I mean…" He shook his head. "Thank you for your help, but I can take it from here."

Ugh!

"Erik." I fought to keep my voice steady. "I'm a *sorceress.* I can take care of myself perfectly well, I assure you."

"I don't doubt it," he replied, sounding frustrated. "Are you always this stubborn?"

I stared at him, saying nothing. A confusing mixture of pleasure and irritation flooded through me when I locked eyes with him. I stayed cool; patient. He clenched his jaw, his gaze heated.

I held on until he gave a huff of defeat and threw up his hands, glaring at the opposite wall.

"Fine," he muttered.

"Fine," I echoed, pleased. It looked like I had won that round.

So what if he didn't want me for a wife? I could be useful to him in other ways.

I ignored the stab of pain at the thought that I would serve this king just as I had my late husband—as a tool to further the betterment of the kingdom. Nothing more.

Erik stalked out of the room. I watched him leave in my

peripheral vision. Presumably, he was off to find somewhere to brood until it was time to leave. I sighed internally and sank down into the nearest chair. My victory lasted all of ten seconds, before it occurred to me precisely *what* I'd signed up for: a carriage journey across a frozen tundra. Alone, for days on end, with the man I craved with every fiber of my being.

This should be interesting.

Erik

STAVROK —

I HAVE REASON TO BELIEVE THAT MY CLAN IS IN GRAVE DANGER. MARIENNE HAD A VISION: OUR CASTLE BURNING, OUR PEOPLE DEAD IN THE STREETS. SHE BELIEVES THAT KING DAMON IS PLANNING AN ATTACK. WHATEVER WE DISCOVER, I'M SURE YOU CAN APPRECIATE THE URGENCY OF THE SITUATION. I'M DETERMINED TO GET TO THE HEART OF IT; OTHERWISE, I'M AFRAID MY REIGN MIGHT BE OVER BEFORE IT HAS EVEN STARTED.

MARIENNE AND I ARE TRAVELLING NORTH TO ASSESS THE SITUATION. WE WANT TO SCOUT DAMON'S KINGDOM BEFORE TAKING ANY ACTION. I HAVE INSTRUCTED MAGNIK'S ARMY—MY ARMY—TO REMAIN ON STANDBY UNTIL OUR RETURN.

THIS ISN'T YOUR FIGHT. BUT IF YOU MEANT WHAT YOU SAID THE LAST TIME WE MET—ABOUT OUR ALLIANCE—I THOUGHT IT BEST THAT YOU KNOW WHAT'S COMING.

I PRAY WE MEET AGAIN UNDER BETTER CIRCUMSTANCES.

ERIK

CONSCIOUS OF OUR TIME CONSTRAINTS, I'd written the letter while sitting in the carriage, so the handwriting wasn't great, but I think I got the message across.

I scanned the letter several times until I was satisfied that I'd said everything I wanted. With a grunt, I pulled the signet ring off my finger and pressed it into the inkpad that lay beside the paper. My signature was marked with my family seal, the royal crest emblazoned on the thick parchment.

The ring was a heavy, silver thing. It had been Magnik's, and my father's before him. And his father's. And on and on.

In moments of boredom or distraction I often found myself twisting it back and forth, uncomfortable with its presence on my finger. After stamping the letter, I wiped the ink off the ring and slipped it back on, making a fist while I waited for the bright ink to dry.

Then I folded the letter into quarters and rapped on the closed carriage door. The door opened, and my butler Thomas hovered outside. "Sire?"

I placed the letter into his hand. "See that this gets to Stavrok," I said, and he gave a short nod.

The cold blast of air into the carriage made a shiver run down my spine, and I yanked the door closed again.

The wind was picking up in earnest, and I wanted to get as far as possible before nightfall. I rapped on the roof of the carriage, and the driver shouted a reply. The horses whinnied as the wheels began to turn, and soon we were well on our way, trundling through the castle grounds at speed.

We had a procession behind us. A sleigh with our possessions and two additional carriages for my men. A small contingent of my army.

I chanced a glance at the seat opposite me.

Marienne sat with her hands folded in her lap. She was staring out at the changing scenery as it passed: dark mountains, trees, the small twinkling lights of the town below us. We weren't going that way, however; we were taking the road that wound up the rockface. The track was narrow and uneven, seldom used by travelers. It wasn't well-maintained, and the carriage wheels jolted over every pothole and lump of gravel.

Perhaps the kingdom should have paid to repair this road, rather than furnish gold chains around the elders' necks.

Marienne didn't seem uncomfortable to be sharing a carriage in dead silence. Her face appeared smooth and peaceful.

I left her alone with her thoughts. I couldn't think what to say.

An apology might be a good start.

A guilty prickle traveled up the back of my neck. It wasn't *her* fault she was saddled with me, after all.

The carriage was silent save for the whistling wind and the occasional distant rockfall. Unable to help myself, I continued to steal glances at her. Something in my chest tightened when my eyes tracked over her long, black hair. It was glossy, and looked almost blue in the shadows, like raven's wings. I remembered how soft it was to touch. A lock fell over her face, framing her jewel-bright eyes.

"Can I help you?"

Her voice startled me, and my cheeks heated with the realization I'd been caught out. I was too dazed to think up a good excuse. "I was just... hoping you packed for the weather."

I gestured lamely to the white skin showing above her low-necked blouse. She arched a delicate eyebrow, and I huffed, looking away.

What was I doing? We were going to be stuck like this for days.

Still, I was struck with a desire to fill the silence. If we couldn't be civil, we could at least use this time to talk tactics.

"We should be smart about this." I ran a hand over my jaw and noted absently that her eyes tracked the movement. "There's no point going in half-cocked. Just in case your visions..."

"They're not wrong," she snapped. "I know what I saw."

"I'm not *saying* they're wrong," I said, before brushing a hand through my hair. "We *are* mounting this expedition up north based on your visions, after all."

Her lips pressed together, before she finally nodded. "All right. I'll give you that."

"Look," I said. "There's too much at stake here—"

"You think I don't know what's at stake? If we don't act now, it will be too late!"

"Unless we get the full picture, we won't even know who our enemy is!" I growled, narrowing my eyes.

Opposite me, Marienne mirrored my posture. We both leaned in close, getting right into each other's space. The air between us simmered with heat.

Outside, the wind picked up. It was howling now, and large white flakes thudded against the glass of the carriage windows, building a thick white layer over the ledge. Snarling, I yanked the velvet curtain across the window to keep in some of the heat. Marienne's flimsy sleeves didn't look like they would provide much protection.

We lapsed back into prickly silence.

The carriage thundered on for a few more miles. The sky outside was dark with snowfall, and I found myself worrying about the remainder of the journey.

I'd never traveled so far north before. I'd heard tales, of course, but I had no idea what to expect.

Ravenous wolves. Frostbite, culminating in a slow, icy death.

Death at the end of a thick iron broadsword.

I wasn't afraid for myself as much as the woman sitting opposite me. Though we were now merely allies—and even *that* label seemed to be hanging by a thread—the thought that I was unknowingly leading her into danger was too much to bear.

For all I knew, we were playing right into Damon's hands.

The carriage wheels ground to a halt, wrenching me from my thoughts. I made eye contact with Marienne when she looked up at the delay. Our gazes darted away from each other, but it was clear her puzzlement equaled mine.

Why have we stopped?

The plan was to travel until we lost the daylight, then make camp. Unless...

I knocked a couple of times on the roof of the carriage, then slid over and opened the door a crack. The blizzard outside raged and a few stray snowflakes snuck through the gap. I craned my neck, squinting up at the driver. He dismounted and hurried toward the horses.

I called out to him. "What's going on?"

"The carriage won't make it any further in this, sire." He indicated the snow that was piling up against the wheels. "I'm afraid you and the queen will have to travel to your camp another way."

My alarm increased with every word he spoke. "What do you mean, another way?"

"The wheels won't make it through the pass in these conditions. You'll have to make the rest of the journey by sleigh."

Through the swirling whiteness that half-blinded me, I looked in the direction he was pointing. The snow was getting deeper by the minute.

Behind us, the small retinue of men that had followed us in a second and third carriage, began unfastening the ropes of the sleigh that carried our meager belongings behind the procession. The horses were led around and harnessed to the sleigh, and I glared out at the howling wilderness before ducking my head back into the carriage.

My eyes widened. From somewhere, Marienne had produced a thick cloak with a high fur collar, complete with a muff. She drew the garments around her small frame and gave me a short nod.

"Are you sure you want to do this?" I murmured. "You could still turn back."

She shook her head. Her eyes betrayed no hint of nervousness, but her face was paler than usual. Without thinking, I reached out and took the small hand that extended from her thick cloak. She clutched at me tightly, betraying her concern as clearly as her pale cheeks.

Without another word, I led us out into the storm.

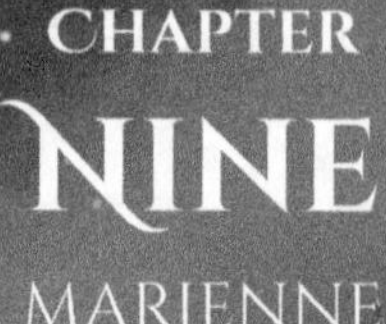

CHAPTER

NINE

MARIENNE

The snow outside fell continuously. I pressed myself up against Erik's side, using his body to shield myself from the worst of the wind as we hurried toward the sleigh.

The conveyance was much smaller than our carriage, but the men had lit the lanterns that hung inside the compartment, giving it a coziness that I gravitated toward.

Golden light spilled out over the snowdrift when Erik opened the door of the sleigh carriage. His hands found my waist, boosting me up, and I clambered inside, glad to be out of the elements.

Erik lingered outside. I listened to him exchange a few words with the men in a low, urgent voice, and then he slipped in behind me and fastened the door.

The crimson cushions inside were comfortable enough, but I came to the awkward realization we would have to share the bench. It was about the size of a loveseat, and Erik's large frame crowded up against mine no matter how we positioned ourselves.

He grunted, and his large hands curled around the horses'

reins. He gave them a sharp tug and we were on the move once more.

"The men will rejoin us once the snow starts easing up," Erik muttered. He stared ahead, his jaw tight and his eyes like flint.

We traveled in silence. Dark, craggy rocks loomed on either side as we approached the pass, and I shivered, grateful for my thick furs.

He huffed, eyes flicking over my form. "Are you cold?"

I shook my head. The little nook had already warmed up due to our shared body heat.

Erik didn't say anything. His eyes were fixed on the road ahead, but I thought I felt him press a little closer.

"You keep asking me that," I whispered, eventually. I couldn't help myself. Despite his obvious lack of interest in me, he still showed the decency to ask if I was all right. "No one ever asked me things like that before you came along."

He shifted in his seat. "It's common courtesy."

"Well, I've lived a very uncommon life." My voice was soft, quiet, but I got the sense that he was hanging on every word. As if he *cared*.

"Yeah?"

"I'm not used to people asking *about* me," I said. "Usually, they want something *from* me. Magnik..."

His name hung in the air between us. I gave a deep sigh, relaxing into the cushions and the warmth of Erik's body.

"I was useful to him." I bit my lip. "But he never trusted me. Not completely. Even when I was a girl, the townsfolk always knew that I... I was... different."

Erik was silent. My heart thudded in my chest. Had I read the situation wrong? Then he reached out, and I found myself lifted and rearranged, so my back pressed against his torso, firm even through all the layers separating us. He tucked his huge arms around me, taking the reins up in his free hand.

"Well, then." He gave my shoulders a gentle squeeze. "I guess we have that in common, Your Majesty."

The tension that had built up between us started to thaw.

Your Majesty.

That title again, which he had said so scornfully the day before... now, it fell from his lips like a pet name.

Something shifted. Despite the storm, and the great, shadowy unknown that loomed from the other side of the mountain range, I felt a kernel of warmth spark inside my chest.

Lulled by the rhythmic sway of the sleigh ride, the thump of Erik's heart beneath my ear, and the whistle of the wind outside, I drifted off into sleep.

I woke to Erik's murmuring voice. My face was pressed against something firm and warm, and I curved in closer, sighing happily.

Once I realized what I was doing in my half-conscious state, I froze.

Blinking rapidly, I withdrew, brushing my tangled hair off my cheeks. The sleigh had stopped moving and Erik turned to me. A smile lingered at the corners of his mouth.

"Ah, Sleeping Beauty is back with us."

I scowled and rubbed at my eyes, straightening up. "How long was I out?"

"About thirty minutes." He paused, his eyes lingering over my face. "We've made it to camp."

Camp, I deduced, as I peered out of the window, was a small log cabin built into the mountainside. The snow had thankfully stopped for the time being, but it was over a foot deep in some places.

Erik held out his arms. "I'll carry you, if you wish. It'll save you from getting those dainty little shoes of yours damp."

I shook my head, cheeks heating up. "I'm sure I'll manage."

With a boyish grin, he flung open the door and pulled me out of the sleigh, his large hands curving around my waist. Before I could protest, he threw me over one shoulder and began wading through the snow toward the cabin.

"Erik!" I closed my fingers around the hair at the nape of his neck, and gave it a sharp tug to express my displeasure.

He let out a yelp before bursting into laughter.

Despite the depth of the snow, Erik got the door to the cabin open, and we tumbled through the doorway in a flurry of snow and tangled limbs. I righted myself and gave him a shove, and he held his hands up, still smiling at me with that crooked, unrepentant smile of his.

"See, your feet are still dry!" He pointed down, and I huffed, unable to deny that he was right. "I'll see to the horses and get them under shelter, and then let's get this place warmed up, shall we?"

While he strode off, I took stock of our surroundings.

The cabin was a simple, one room dwelling, with an adjoining bathroom, and a lean-to at the side where Erik would presumably lead the horses.

A heavy iron stove crouched in the corner, and snowshoes hung in the rafters over the one tiny bed.

Hanging in the corner was a rough-hewn, wooden cradle. I kept away from it, focusing my attention on the narrow bed and the rocking chair with the patchwork quilt thrown over it.

When Erik returned with kindling, he quickly started a fire for the stove while I set one in the hearth. In no time, the room began to warm up.

"Erik?"

"Hmm?"

I turned from the fireplace to see him poking at the stove,

which now flickered and glowed. He handed me a piece of bread and I took it.

"Whoever chose this place didn't think very hard about our sleeping arrangements," I said wryly.

His eyes followed my gaze to the tiny bed. It was barely big enough for one person, let alone someone of Erik's size.

He chewed on his piece of bread for a beat or two, before swallowing. "I'll take the chair."

"Oh." Something inside my chest curled. "No. It's... You can't..."

There was that crooked grin again. The one that made my heart turn over in my chest.

"Marienne." He reached out and put a hand on my shoulder. "It's not a discussion."

We stared at each other.

Eventually, I sighed. "Very well."

We ate in companionable silence, positioned close to the stove. Erik even made me a hot coffee, which warmed me as we sat there. The crackling logs filled the cabin with a smoky smell, and I relaxed into it.

How was it that here, in the middle of nowhere with a man I barely knew, I felt safer than I had in... forever?

I laughed when Erik gathered up the quilt and draped it around his shoulders, posing in a mock-heroic stance, his arms crossed over his broad chest.

"Your Highness." I bowed low, accepting his outstretched hand.

He pressed a kiss to the back of my knuckles. For a moment, I forgot we were play-acting, and my breath caught as his mouth touched my skin.

He dropped my hand, and the laughter died from his eyes as he slumped back into the chair. I perched on the end of the bed, studying him. In the low light, all traces of the stoic warrior I had traveled with vanished. He looked like the young man he was, his hair rumpled, his shoulders set with unease.

"What you said earlier..." He looked up at me, and my gaze dropped. "About growing up... It was like that for me, too. I was always the strongest. The first boy my age to shift. My village didn't know who I truly was, but they could tell I was different."

"It wasn't right," I whispered. "Your father should have raised you in the castle. You were his son, his *blood*. It was your birthright."

He ran a hand through his hair and shrugged. "If that were the case, Magnik wouldn't have allowed me to live."

As much as I hated hearing that, I knew he was likely right.

His eyes met mine, his gaze lit by and reflecting the heat of the flames. "All I'm saying is, I know how it feels, Mari. To be misunderstood. To have people look at you like..."

He waved a hand. *He called me Mari.* I liked the sound of the nickname Lucy had given me, on Erik's lips. I smiled at him, and finished the sentence he'd started.

"Like you're a powder keg waiting to explode?"

He looked at me sharply. "Exactly." His serious expression melted away.

"I guess it's about finding the balance, right?" I wrapped my hands around the warm mug, breathing in the steam.

"How do you mean?"

"Well..." I paused, listening to the fire crackle. "I'm a sorceress, but I'm also a woman."

His eyes flickered over my face. I saw what he was imagining clear enough, and a heat rose in my cheeks.

"I don't mean like *that*. I just mean..." I bit my lip. "My power doesn't mean I'm some kind of heartless *force*. It's part of me, but I'm not driven by it. I want things just like any other woman. Love, companionship..."

Children. I trailed off once I realized what I was about to admit.

Erik gazed at me, his expression unreadable. I shook my head, letting the hair fall over my face to hide my blush.

"The way I see it, your shifter is the same as my magic." I inhaled deeply, breathing in the intoxicating combination of woodsmoke and the heady scent of Erik next to me. "It's part of you, so close that you couldn't imagine life without it. But... you're more than just the dragon, Erik. And I'm so much more than my magic."

He huffed, dropping his head down. My eyes traced over the broad span of his shoulders. In the firelight, the muscles in his back were particularly defined; they showed through his thin undershirt in a manner I found distracting.

"Never thought that you and I could have so much in common." He lifted his head and stared at me. My breath hitched at the look in his eyes.

I wanted him so badly. It would be easy, *too* easy, to lean in and kiss him.

But I had to respect his wishes. The bond between us was undeniable, but I could ignore it. I had to. I couldn't tempt him into losing control again, no matter how hungrily he was gazing at me.

"I guess there's a lot we don't know about each other," I said eventually, glancing up at him through my eyelashes.

"I guess so."

We laughed a little, our eyes lingering over each other, soft and warm. Heat coiled in my stomach.

It was a far cry from where we had started out that morning. Being away from the castle changed everything. All the tension and insecurity had fallen away, dropped somewhere along the road that lay behind us.

In some ways, I wanted it to go on like this forever.

Nevertheless, I couldn't suppress a yawn when it came. I pressed the back of my hand against my open mouth, but Erik wasn't fooled. His voice softened, low and quiet against the roar of the wind outside.

"You should get some rest."

I got up and lit the lantern, then carried it to the bedside. "You're sure you don't want to take the bed?"

He shrugged the quilt over his shoulders and nodded. "I'm used to roughing it, Majesty. Besides, I wouldn't fit in that thing in a million years."

I shook my head at him, but I couldn't argue with his logic. The bed was pretty small.

I slipped out of my shoes and pulled my long stockings down, folding them neatly and hanging them over the foot of the bed. Erik turned his face away, staring at the flames: ridiculous behavior, given the fact that he'd seen everything already.

I slid between the sheets, too tired to bother with night-clothes. I curled up on my side, my mind drifting already.

I studied his large frame in silhouette against the glow from the stove. It made for a comforting picture. The image of Erik grew more and more hazy as my eyelids fought to stay open. I was exhausted, but I didn't care.

Now that he was in my life, I wanted to look at him for as long as possible.

It was stupid, and irrational, but I couldn't shake the feeling that, if I closed my eyes and fell asleep, he might disappear forever.

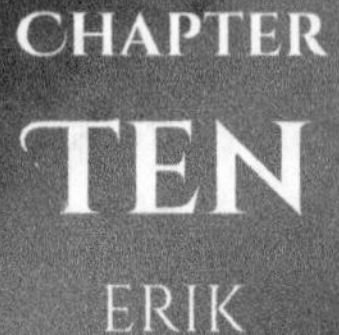

I woke to a sore back and a crick in my neck.

Groaning, I pulled myself up out of the rocking chair that had been my bed for the night and grimaced as I folded the quilt.

I'd had worse nights.

Marienne was stretched out on the little cot, fast asleep. Her dark hair feathered out over the pillow, framing her peaceful face.

I had a crazy impulse to lean down and place a kiss on her sleeping mouth, like a prince in a fairytale. After a minute, I snorted to myself and shook away the thought, moving to the window.

Last night had been strange, to say the least. I was glad we were on friendly terms again, even if my heart wouldn't stop racing every time she came near.

Now I knew about the bond between us, I could rationalize it to myself. It must be the dragon that slumbered under my skin that hungered for her, not *me*. Every urge I had, every impulse to wrap my hands around her hips and pull her against me... it was all down to him. My dragon.

I glanced at her sleeping form.

I had to admit, though, our relationship was more complicated now. It wasn't lust crowding everything else out of my mind.

I actually *liked* her.

Gods, I had to focus. Like it or not, we had more pressing matters to deal with than my idiotic feelings.

Outside, the world was a bright, sparkling white. Mercifully, it hadn't snowed much more in the night, which would ease our journey considerably.

Sleepy murmurs sounded from across the room, and I looked over my shoulder to find Marienne staring at me shyly.

"Good morning." Her mouth curled upwards, sweet, pink, and tempting as sin.

I mumbled something in reply as I fumbled for my jacket and boots and shoved them on. She watched me as I trudged out the door, but I didn't look back.

Everything in me wanted to sweep her up into my arms and ravish her completely.

I had to get out of there before I did something I wasn't certain she wanted.

The horses whinnied in greeting as I checked them over, tending to them in preparation for the day ahead. If we made good progress, we should reach our destination by nightfall.

I stroked my hand down a horse's flank, gentling it. Truth be told, I was more at home out here than I was in the castle. *This* was the life in which I had been raised. It might be simple, but it was what I knew.

I glanced back toward the mountain pass. Behind us lay my castle. More council meetings, more jargon I couldn't get my head around. More petty power struggles and diplomatic entanglements.

I looked the other way, down the road we were traveling. I had no idea what lay around the corner, but it couldn't be good.

Marienne appeared at my side. She had changed into a thick fur coat and hat, and her hair hung in a long braid over her shoulder.

Her eyes traveled to my hands, as I went over the horses' tack again.

"You're good at that." She nodded in the direction of the horse, fiddling with the end of her braid.

I smiled. "It's what I know."

"Animals have always been nervous around me." Despite her words, she drew closer, like she couldn't help herself. "It's because of my magic, I think. They can sense it."

The horse huffed when Marienne came up alongside me. I hushed it until it calmed down and held out my hand.

Her eyes flicked up at me, long lashes shadowing her cheeks. I wiggled my fingers, and with a sigh she slid her palm against mine.

Gently, I turned her hand around and shadowed it with mine. We approached the horse together.

"If you're scared," I said, my voice ruffling the soft strands of hair around her ear, "they can tell. But if you're nice and calm... there, see?"

Her hand stroked along the horse's mane. The horse shuffled its feet a little but remained calm, allowing her to pet it without complaint. Marienne breathed out in amazement and my heart swelled in my chest.

Eventually, she drew away and gazed up at me. Her eyes were even more striking in contrast with the snow, but it was her expression that made her truly radiant. She looked so happy, all of a sudden.

"Thank you." She reached out and squeezed my hand, and I squeezed back before I could think better of it.

"We should make a move," I muttered, pulling away from her and heading back to the cabin to grab our supplies.

She bobbed along by my side.

"Not before I get some food into you." She nudged me out of the way at the door, batting her eyelashes at me over her shoulder. "Sire."

"Has anyone ever told you," I called after her, "for a royal subject, you're quite cheeky?"

"I think you'd be the first, Your Highness!"

I laughed, shaking my head. "I find that hard to believe."

THE BUOYANT MOOD drained away once we were on the road again.

Once the snowstorm cleared, we made good progress, but the further we journeyed, the closer we were to enemy territory.

Around mid-morning, we made it through the mountains. They loomed up behind us, stretching into the pale sky. For the first time, I sensed how truly vulnerable we were, just two people, heading into the vast unknown.

The procession would catch up with us once they found a way through the snow. But they were probably half a day behind us.

Marienne's hand found mine in the space between us, and our fingers tangled together.

Just yesterday, I had been terrified for her safety. I couldn't help but be glad she was here now. Whatever we found at Winter Castle, we would face it together.

Small farmsteads appeared on the horizon. The landscape was flat and sparse, and the settlements were bleak places without trees, or crops, or even signs of fire or life.

I shuddered to think of the life of pure survival the people in this place must live. Dragon shifters were a tall, proud people, and they needed a lot of food to survive.

How does this clan manage?

The snow drifted around us as we trundled through the frozen wasteland. We were nearing our checkpoint, where we would meet with the members of the expedition we had been forced to abandon in yesterday's snowstorm.

There was a rocky ridge up ahead. The back of my neck prickled as I drew the sleigh to a standstill.

Beside me, Marienne tensed. We exchanged glances and emerged from the sleigh together, sticking close to each other as we inched forward through the snow.

I didn't bother telling her to stay put. I would be wasting my breath.

I glanced up, something glinting in the sunlight on the ridge catching my eye. It was the shiny edge of an axe. The blood froze in my veins. These weren't our men. This was an ambush.

A raven wheeled in the sky overhead. Its sharp cry pierced through my chest. My heart thumped, and my head filled with white noise. Marienne whispered something to me in an urgent voice, but I didn't catch it. I had failed before the game had even started. I'd led us both into a trap, and we were about to pay the price.

"Put up your hands!" A male voice from behind me sounded, low and guttural. "Both of you!"

Slowly, I raised my hands. One glance via my peripheral vision told me that there were more soldiers behind us, bristling with weapons.

We were surrounded by the toughest men I'd ever seen. They were all huge, wearing long coats of fur suitable for their weather and they carried large weapons. Axes and swords aplenty.

Beside me, Marienne's eyes glowed with magic. I knew she was waiting for my signal. One look from me, and she would start throwing fireballs. Some buried instinct told me to wait.

They haven't attacked us. There's a reason for that; there has to be.

Instead, the men simply stood, tensed for action. But still, they didn't approach.

"I am King Bravadik of the Black Mountains. I've come here with Dowager Queen Marienne," I said, with all the confidence I didn't feel. "I wish to speak with King Damon."

If they so much as looked sideways at Marienne, I would transform into my dragon and fight our way out of here. But at the moment, my instincts were telling me to go along with the guards and find out exactly what was going on in this strange kingdom to the north.

Only time would tell if I'd been right to follow those instincts, or not.

Marienne

FOR THE REST of the journey to Damon's castle, we traveled under armed guard.

Or, as I tried to think of it, a royal escort.

I held my head high, pretending for all the world that we'd been expecting this. If my years as Magnik's queen had taught me one thing, it was never to show fear in front of your enemy.

My response didn't seem to matter either way. Our captors barely glanced at me. They surrounded us on all sides, stone-faced, their focus purely on Erik. They were covered in thick furs, and their massive, hulking frames made it difficult for me to see the castle up ahead as we approached it.

By my side, Erik's profile was firm, unmoving, but his jaw was clenched tight. I could tell that it was taking every ounce of his concentration not to shift and fly us both out of there.

My magic simmered through my veins, sensing the threat that dragged us further and further into dangerous territory. But I knew better than to strike out at our captors. If I lost control, it would spell disaster for us all. War would break out between our clans, and all my visions—all the fire, bloodshed, and death—would come true. And it would be all my fault.

A huge black shape loomed out of the snowdrifts, dominating the skyline. Tall towers spiked upward, and the heavy iron gates of the drawbridge clanked open as we approached. Ravens perched along the high stone walls. They watched our progress with beady, inquisitive eyes.

I shivered. I could feel it in my bones; the birds were a bad omen.

As we trundled over the drawbridge, I caught flickers of movement from the parapets. How many people were hidden beyond these high walls? An army?

More to the point, the guards were totally silent. Almost sullen. Not what I expected from men who had captured such a powerful enemy.

As we climbed the uneven steps up to the entrance, Erik offered me his arm. I took it, half-amused that he was finally remembering court etiquette at a time like this, half-grateful I wouldn't slip and lose my footing on the icy stone.

We entered a huge, dark hallway. I shook the snow from my hair, glad to be out of the elements. My eyes struggled to adjust to the gloom; the man who seemed to lead the others held up a lantern, and in the soft light I could make out vague, dark shapes.

There were long, jagged cracks in the wooden beams that held up the ceiling. Cobwebs trailed from heavy candelabras above our heads, and all along the wall, pale squares suggested that paintings and tapestries had been torn down.

Huh.

All in all, it wasn't that different from our castle, or Stavrok's, but...

This one looked abandoned. Lifeless.

I frowned as we were led deeper inside the castle, through a high archway into a smaller antechamber. The lack of any sign of life didn't make sense. All the fireplaces were dark and empty, and a chilling wind howled through them, giving the place a desolate air.

I shuddered. I was no warmer now that we were inside. I puffed out a few breaths, noting the white clouds that formed.

"Something's wrong," I murmured to Erik. He tilted his head down so I could whisper directly into his ear. "Why is it so dark?"

We reached a set of ornately carved doors. Wolves and dragons intertwined in the dark grain, and I leaned in, impressed by the beauty of the artwork. But even here, once I got closer, I noted the scratches and cuts that marred the surface of the wood.

Dragon claws?

Erik pressed me further into his side and I tried to muffle the automatic sigh of relief at the feel of his strong body against mine.

Even now, when we were literally about to brave the lair of the beast, it felt so right to be with Erik.

Without a word or a backward glance at us, the guard strode forward and knocked on the door.

"Your Majesty. You have guests. King Bravadik of the Black Mountains, and Dowager Queen Marienne."

My chest tingled at the sound of our names. Spoken together like that, they sounded... good.

I hung my head, feeling foolish for having such a thought at a time like this.

"Enter."

The voice behind the door was low, but it pierced through the wooden door clear as crystal. The fear that I had managed to quell rose again, stronger than ever.

We were nudged forward by the guards, and the doors opened on either side of us, revealing a small room. Thankfully, this one had a small fire burning in the grate.

If we're about to be murdered, at least it'll be somewhere marginally warm.

Erik and I inched forward. The doors shut behind us with a final rush of cold air. We were both on high alert for any sign of sudden movement.

But none came. The room was just... a perfectly ordinary room. Half-office, half-sitting room, with a large oil painting over the fireplace and messy stacks of paperwork scattered over every available surface.

A lived-in room, unlike the rest of the castle.

We glanced at each other. Erik looked as puzzled as I did.

"Hello?" I called out, cautiously.

Something stirred at the large desk, behind stacks of papers. As one, we whirled to face it. Erik closed his hand over my arm, firm and protective.

Damon sat in a chair by the desk. I'd met him at several king's council dinners, but never truly spoken to him. He was tall and broad, like Erik, and his eyes were like ice. He wasn't old, and yet his hair was threaded with silver.

King Damon stared at us, and we stared back, too much in shock at his ravaged appearance to speak.

This was the man who had haunted my nightmares for days. And yet...

He didn't look like someone planning an attack. Dark shadows circled his eyes, and his huge frame was bowed inwards, like he had the weight of the world on his shoulders. He looked exhausted, almost ill.

What was going on here?

"Marienne." His voice was gravelly, like he didn't use it all that much these days. "It's nice to see you again."

I chose my words carefully. Even if it didn't seem like we were in immediate danger, we couldn't relax. I had lived through my entire marriage to Magnik on the edge of a tightrope. The threat of the dungeons always lurked in the back of my mind. I knew how to play the game.

Inclining my head, I emerged slightly from Erik's side so I could address Damon properly. "Your Majesty. It's been too long."

"And you decided to pay me a visit, it seems." Damon's eyes flicked to Erik. "With your new king. You're Magnik's half-brother?"

"That's right." Erik spoke evenly, but the forearm I was still gripping was tense. "They crowned me a week ago."

"Congratulations." Damon bowed his head. When he looked up, his pale eyes regarded us with an unreadable expression. "I'm sorry I couldn't make it to the ceremony."

"I won't hold it against you," Erik said, indicating the mess spread over the desk. "It looks like you have your hands full here."

His voice was conversational, diplomatic. I was impressed. This was a strange and unsettling place, and the odds were not stacked in our favor, but Erik was leading the conversation like we were chatting with friends over dinner.

The ghost of a smile crept over Damon's face. He looked down at the chaos, and then back up to us, arching a brow.

"You're not much like him, are you?"

Erik took half a step forward. "Who?"

"Your brother. Magnik." Damon glanced at me, then returned his gaze to Erik. "You don't seem very much like your father, either."

"I wouldn't know," Erik said. "I never met either of them, beyond having them pointed out to me by my mother."

King Damon circled around the desk, moving toward us with his hands behind his back. He walked slowly, casually, like we'd been invited here. Like we hadn't been marched to this room under guard.

I couldn't let myself forget that fact, no matter how friendly his manner. I squeezed Erik's arm, and he flicked a glance my way. His mouth was tight, and he gave me a tiny nod.

ELEVEN

ERIK

"I wish I could say I'd never met my father..." Damon trailed off with a sigh. I followed the line of his gaze, up to the painting that hung over the fireplace.

A fearsome-looking man stared back. He had Damon's pale, ice-blue eyes, but that was where the resemblance ended. His face was longer, and his jawline narrower. His expression was pinched, and his mouth had been painted with a cruel, foreboding twist.

The northern kings were known to be reclusive. They kept to themselves all year round. Nobody thought anything of it.

When Damon inherited the throne, none of the other clans had been present.

Were Erik and I the first outsiders to visit his court?

Erik strode forward, moving to stand beside Damon in front of the fireplace. Subtly, I crept away so I could study the documents that lay on the desk.

At a glance, they looked normal enough. Balance sheets. Payment notices.

"Did you not get along with your father?" Erik asked.

There was a long pause as Damon seemed to ponder his answer.

"My father ruled this clan like the tyrant he was." He spoke into the fireplace, gazing at the flames like they might reveal their secrets to him. "He drove my mother into an early grave. He cut off our clan from all outside influences. In his eyes, every other kingdom was a threat to his power."

Damon's words made me shiver. Memories of all the long years I'd spent at Magnik's side, helpless to stop his cruel nature, stirred up inside me. I may have been his wife, but to all intents and purposes I had been a prisoner in a gilded cage in my tower, subject like all of us in the kingdom to the whims of a power-hungry king...

Had Magnik been a tyrant, like Damon's father? Not quite, perhaps, but certainly close enough.

"Toward the end, his gambling got worse and worse." Damon practically spat out the words. "We lost so much. The castle fell to ruin, as you've probably already noticed, but even that wasn't enough for him. He raised taxes and drained the wealth from our land, all to feed his addiction."

He whirled around and strode over to the window, looking out at the barren, wintery landscape. "But all the money in the north couldn't settle the debts he racked up. Our whole clan is starving. Debtors took our entire crop yield, and it wasn't enough. They want blood and will be back for our heads by the end of the month. We are done for. The whole clan. There is nothing left."

My mind spiraled with the shock of his words. I stared blankly at the whirling snowflakes outside, a new realization dawning.

The visions hadn't been wrong, but they hadn't shown the full picture.

A burning castle. People dead in the street.

All this time, I had thought that it was *our* castle under siege. Our people in mortal danger.

I had been given fragments of a puzzle and put the pieces together as best I could. But I'd been wrong. And I had led Erik here, right into the heart of the danger.

Damon turned, standing framed in the window. From this angle he looked like a young, grim reflection of his father's painting.

"When my guards spotted you in the distance, I thought the other kingdoms had heard of our misfortune. We feared you had sent spies to check our defenses for weaknesses before sending in your army." He spread out his hands,. "Imagine my surprise when I was told it was the king and queen themselves, in the flesh."

"Why are you telling us this?" Erik asked, uncertainty in his tone.

Damon shrugged, his eyes hollow and blank. "Why not? I don't know why you've come, but it doesn't matter much to me, either way. Our clan is finished." His mouth twisted as he looked up at his father's portrait. "My father never thought much of my chances after I took the throne. It seems he was right. I'll forever be known as the king who destroyed the royal line of Ice Dragons."

"But..." I burst out.

The two men turned to look at me, and my cheeks heated.

"With respect, Your Majesty," I said, "we are only here because we thought you were planning to wage war on *us*."

Damon's brow furrowed. "Why would you... ah." His face cleared as comprehension dawned. "The sorceress of the Black Mountains. The rumors of your skill at sorcery were not exaggerated, then."

"They weren't," Erik said. He spared a glance at me, then moved to stand beside me so he could also study the documents on the desk.

I stepped away from him, drawing Damon's attention, and drew my arms around my waist, suddenly self-conscious.

"I don't know about that. The visions, they're not always under my control. A few days ago, I saw... you." I glanced around at the desolate room, then out at the snowstorm. "I saw horrors I can't even explain. I thought..."

The memory of Erik in my arms, the life leaving his body, filled me with a wave of grief that almost choked me.

"Forgive me, Your Majesty," I said. "I thought you were responsible. We traveled here because we had to know for sure. We had to at least try to avert war, if we could."

"It was brave of you to come all this way." Damon's eyes softened as he stared between us. "So far from everything you know. The southern clans don't usually bother themselves with us. It's a rare thing, to venture this far north beyond the mountains."

All these years, the northern kingdom had been the stuff of legend. Spoken about in whispers, in dark tales full of ice monsters with sharp claws and sharper teeth.

I now saw the loner king in a different light. Up close, he was just another young man thrust under the burden of leadership, trying to follow in the footsteps of a tyrant.

Damon and Erik had more in common than any of us had realized.

"Well." Damon clapped his hands together, interrupting my train of thought. "Now that you know the truth, I expect you'll want to begin the journey home."

I frowned and glanced at Erik, who was looking determined and resolute.

"Home?" I repeated.

Damon looked uncertain. "It's a long way, if I'm not mistaken. You'll want to set off before dark so that you may put as much distance between yourselves and my kingdom as possible."

"Damon." Erik cleared his throat. "With respect, I think I speak for both of us when I say that we'd like to stay here a little longer."

I nodded, moving back to stand beside Erik. Outside, the wind picked up again, howling so loudly it almost drowned out my words.

"We won't abandon you to your fate," I said. "Your people don't deserve to suffer for the sins of the past, and neither do you."

Damon's eyes widened as Erik approached him, moving with authority and grace. If I didn't know better, I would have thought he'd spent his whole life doing this. He didn't seem to know it, but Erik had stepped into the role of king quickly and already presented as a natural-born ruler.

Erik placed a hand over his heart and inclined his head. "I pledge allegiance to the northern dragon clan. I will send for my army at once. You won't fight this battle against your debtors alone."

Damon's mouth flattened into a hard line and his jaw tightened as he considered the proposal. Then, he reached out and grabbed Erik by the forearm. Erik grabbed Damon's arm, and they shook on it in the way of dragon kings, sealing the pact between our kingdoms.

A smile played at the corners of my mouth as I regarded them. This trip had taken an unexpected turn, but the terror that had plagued me for days melted away with the look on Erik's face.

He was capable. Confident. Righteous.

And sexy as hell.

I bit my lip, my thoughts veering off in a direction wholly inappropriate to the situation. Damon and Erik conversed in low voices, and I struggled to keep my thoughts on track when I heard my name.

"Hmm?" I blinked, coming back to the world to find the two men regarding me with amusement.

"We've been traveling for days." Erik turned to Damon. "My— Marienne—is a little tired."

I glared at him, and he threw me a smirk the moment Damon turned away. "I'm listening."

"I was saying that we should go to Stavrok, too. There's strength in numbers." Erik paced over the worn carpet. "I'm certain he will help your cause, Damon."

King Damon looked awe-struck. His mouth was open, his eyes wide. And he was barely blinking. Then he started to shake his head, as though Erik's plan was flawed.

"Stavrok is a good man," I added gently. "He spared my life, once. He will do what's right. I know it."

Damon sighed, and ran a frazzled hand through his hair.

"In that case, your journey will be longer by some distance." Damon glanced out of the window. "And the weather will only get worse, I'm afraid."

"Oh." Erik sauntered toward me, and I couldn't help but grin back. "We won't be traveling back the way we came. Right, Mari?"

We'd taken the carriage to hide from Damon, assuming he was the one responsible for the devastation I saw in my vision. We didn't need to hide Erik's dragon any longer.

My heart raced as I absorbed his use of the nickname Lucy had given me, and the confident way he held himself. Something smoldered behind his eyes, blazing through his body. I felt the pull toward him, always there just under the surface, intensify even further.

My grin widened and I nodded. I wouldn't miss this experience for anything.

Erik's dragon was waking up, and I was about to ride him.

TWELVE

ERIK

It was a whole new experience, flying through a storm like this.

The snow pelted against my wings as we flew hard against the force of the wind. Marienne gripped tight onto my back, and the warmth of her magic spread through my scales and tingled across my chest.

I threw back my head and roared, sending a jet stream of fire into the cold air, and I heard snatches of her delighted laughter before the gale whipped the sound away.

Despite the blizzard, we covered the barren ground in a matter of hours and approached the mountains. I was strong even for a dragon shifter, and my broad wingspan cast long shadows as we moved over the earth below.

I dove low over the mountain range, banking in the air and swooping down into the valley. We passed over our castle, which looked like a child's toy nestled among the black hulking rocks.

Before long, Stavrok's castle emerged from the mists. As we passed through the snowstorm, shafts of sunlight pierced the clouds above us as I flew down toward our destination.

Mari leapt down off my back as I landed, her steps sure and confident as if we had been flying together for years.

As I shifted back to human, I couldn't keep the grin off my face. The woman I had by my side... she was truly extraordinary. She had journeyed with me to the edge of our world and braved the long flight home with no hesitation whatsoever.

She smiled back at me when she caught me looking. Her gaze lingered, trailing lower, and I realized with a jolt *why* her smile became a smirk.

I didn't have time to do anything about my naked and obviously hardening cock, however, because a group of guards were already approaching us. One was carrying an armful of fabric, which I took gratefully.

Once I was robed, we followed them inside, down a maze of hallways and corridors until we found ourselves in a small courtyard.

"Sire," the guard called out to the king as we approached. "You have visitors."

Stavrok turned, grinning broadly at us. I felt less underdressed when I realized he was shirtless, sweaty and disheveled. We'd interrupted his sparring practice.

"Erik!" he boomed, throwing out his arms and striding toward us. "And Marienne, too! I assume you're here about the letter?"

He reached out and swept Marienne into a tight hug, his broad arms around her slim waist. She looked taken-aback but accepted the hug with a peal of soft laughter.

A sharp wave of irrational anger flooded through me. I itched to pry his hands off her, drag her away from him...

It didn't make any sense. Stavrok was a friend, and I knew he wasn't a threat. He'd never hurt Marienne. So why was I glaring a hole in the side of his head?

Before I could think on it further, Stavrok pulled back and barked with laughter at the look on my face.

"Don't worry, Erik." He clapped a broad hand on my shoulder. "You can tell your dragon to stand down. I'm happily married."

I shuffled on my feet, awkward in his presence. Up until now, I had been certain of myself and my instincts, but... standing here, I was thrown. The whole journey to the north already felt like a lifetime ago.

Mari's small, soft hand slipped into mine and squeezed. I looked down; she smiled up at me softly.

I smiled back. Just having her by my side was enough to cool the protective instincts that threatened to swallow me whole.

I turned to Stavrok, my gaze sobering. "Marienne and I have just returned from the north. I decided to come straight here and meet with you in person."

Stavrok's face was grave; it wasn't an expression I associated with such a jovial man.

"I read your letter. You were right to reach out to me. Whatever Marienne's visions mean, they likely concern all of us." He picked up a heavy-looking broadsword that he'd been training with and slung it over his shoulder. "Come on, this isn't a conversation to be had in the yard. Let's find my wife."

With a glance at Marienne, I inclined my head, and we followed Stavrok through the courtyard to the open doors. Before we could go much further, however, Lucy found *us*.

"Mari!" She barreled forward, her blonde waves bouncing behind her. The two women hugged tightly. "Oh my gosh, it's so good to see you!"

"It's been too long." Marienne pulled back, her face shining with affection. "I'm sorry our visit was cut so short last time."

She pointedly did not look at me, but my face heated anyway. I pretended intense interest in the blank stone wall in front of me while Lucy giggled.

"I understand. Come, this way."

She looped her arm through Stavrok's, and the two led us

through the castle corridors, Marienne and I following awkwardly behind.

The memory of my shift prickled hot and uncomfortable around the collar of my robe. Marienne seemed to be remembering it, too. Small spots of color appeared on her cheeks, and she wouldn't meet my gaze.

Lucy opened a door, and we entered a cozy round room with large, floor-length windows. She settled in an armchair and indicated we do the same opposite.

"I've called for some food," she said. "You must be hungry."

As soon as she said the words, my stomach growled. I smiled at her, relaxing onto a long, low sofa. "Indeed. My dragon flew a long way, and I am ravenous."

Mari cleared her throat and I glanced at her, to find her cheeks fully ablaze with pink. Suddenly, remembering the way her legs had gripped my scales and her hands clung to my dragon form as I flew, I was ravenous for something else altogether.

After an awkward moment, broken only by a bark of laughter from Stavrok, I forced my desire for Mari back down and tried to concentrate on the matter at hand.

"So," Stavrok began. "What happened on your northern expedition? Tell us everything."

Between the two of us, Marienne and I managed to relay everything that had happened on our travels, minus a few details here and there. I hoped that *getting captured* wouldn't make it into the history books when they talked of my reign.

Stavrok and Lucy listened attentively.

At some point the food arrived, and we took bites of delicious bread and cheese and drank steaming cups of hot chocolate while we talked. Their eyes grew wider and wider when they heard the truth about Damon, and when Marienne described the state of his kingdom, Lucy laid a hand on Stavrok's arm.

"We have to help them," she said.

"We will, my love." His brow furrowed as he stared off into the middle distance for a moment. "We must."

Lucy shifted, turning to Marienne. "Come and meet our little ones. You haven't had the chance yet, have you?"

She stood up, brushing her skirt down, and Marienne took the opportunity to get away, after a glance in my direction.

I recognized the gesture for what it was. A chance for me and Stavrok to talk, one-on-one. Ruler to ruler.

Smart little human, that Lucy.

Not much seemed to get past her. She may not have been born in this realm, but she fit into it perfectly.

If she can do it, maybe there's hope for me after all.

"So...." Stavrok leaned forward. "It seems that the loner king is nothing like he's rumored to be."

"I suppose it's easy for a king to be misunderstood," I replied, and Stavrok nodded. "My instincts told me he wasn't a threat. I think he's telling the truth."

"I met his father once." Stavrok squinted, like he was trying to recall a vague memory. "At a tournament, a long time ago. He was a brutish man. He hated the other clans and wanted nothing to do with them. Everyone assumed that all northerners followed his example. It seems we were wrong."

"Not all sons turn out like their fathers," I pointed out.

Stavrok chuckled. He lifted his mug, and I clinked it against mine, grinning.

"You've certainly shown that," he said. "I'll fight by your side, Erik. We're allies, and I'm a man of my word."

I bowed my head out of respect, but he shook the gesture off, putting his hands on my shoulders and looking me dead in the eye.

"You are a king, Erik," he said firmly. "It is your birthright, your bloodline. You bow to *no one.* Remember that."

As he spoke, sunlight pierced through the windows behind us

and filled the room with a golden glow. Somehow, his words gave me a sense of purpose, of peace. I hadn't felt such a thing on the day of my coronation, but I felt it now.

I *was* the King of the Black Mountains. I accepted that role, now. And I would defend what was mine until my final, dying breath.

Marienne

I KNEW a ruse when I saw one, but I couldn't be annoyed at Lucy for separating me from Erik for the time being.

It was clear how much Erik respected Stavrok. Besides, it was good for us to be apart. I needed to get my head straight. Especially if we were going to fight this war that was coming, together.

"So," Lucy said, and grinned, leading me up the grand staircase. "Tell me everything."

"About what?" I asked.

"Marienne!" She huffed, slipping her arm through mine as we strode along the hallway. It was sunnier up here, and I tilted my head, grateful to feel the warmth on my face. "Come on. You and Erik!"

I bit my lip to stop the smile that threatened to appear. Lucy was as lively as ever. Her brief stint in Magnik's castle dungeons didn't seem to have dampened her spirit one bit.

"I don't know what you're talking about." I widened my eyes and batted my eyelashes, before breaking into giggles at the look on her face. "Okay, okay!"

"Is he your fated mate?" Lucy asked. "I know you, Marienne. Did you have a vision about him? How long have you known?"

"Whoa!" I held up my hands to stop the deluge of questions. "I've known about him for years. Ever since I saw him one day in the street, as Magnik and I passed through his town in a procession. As soon as I laid eyes on him, I knew."

Lucy's face fell. "Really? That long, and you couldn't..."

I hunched my shoulders as she trailed off. Her expression was full of pity. I didn't want her pity. And yet, I understood it. the thought of the long and lonely years I'd spent as Magnik's queen, knowing my fated mate was out there and I couldn't be with him, still left me hollow inside.

Luckily, I didn't have to change the subject. We had come to a standstill beside a high, arched door. Lucy pushed it open and I gasped as we entered a brightly lit room. Three cradles clustered around a window. Gauzy golden hangings swayed gently in the wind, and tiny mobiles hung from the ceiling.

I drew closer, and my heart softened when I saw that each mobile had tiny dragons hanging from it.

Reaching out one finger, I nudged the dragon in the middle, watching it spin around and catch the light. The baby in the cradle cooed, waving tiny, chubby fists at me.

"They're so precious." I smiled.

Lucy came up alongside me and brushed a hand through the baby's fluffy hair. "This little one is always causing me trouble, aren't you, Anselm? His sisters are good as gold—mostly."

Baby Anselm blinked up at me, and I reached out a hand, swirling a shimmering stream of magic through the air above his head. He gurgled with laughter, reaching up to try and grab the twinkling light before it dissolved.

As the light faded away, so did my smile. My hand fell away, and I traced the edge of the crib, lost in thought.

"For someone who's finally able to be with their fated mate," Lucy said slowly, "you don't seem very happy."

"It isn't that simple." I turned away from the cribs, sighing. "None of it is."

"What do you mean?" Lucy put a hand on my arm. "I've seen the way he looks at you, Mari."

"It's not—it's not like that between us." I ran my hands over my face, hating the way my voice caught in my throat. "It shouldn't be! I'm hardly the perfect match, Lucy."

Lucy snorted. "Well, now you're just talking nonsense. Fated mates are, by definition, perfect for one another."

I held up my hand and counted off the reasons. "I was married for ten years to his half-brother. I'm not a dragon shifter. I don't think I'll ever be able to give him children—I was told years ago that I'm barren, Lucy. And sooner or later, he'll realize he wants someone without all this... this baggage! And of course, he will want an heir, one day."

I raised my hands and let out a sob as purplish mist swirled around me.

Lucy's face softened and she strode forward, sweeping me into a tight hug.

She drew back, wiping the tears from my cheeks. "But you're forgetting the most important thing."

I sniffed. "What's that?"

"He wants *you*, you idiot! It's obvious how crazy you are about each other."

As much as I wanted to believe her, I didn't dare. I cast my eyes downward as I mumbled, "The night he shifted, we slept together."

Lucy's face lit up. "And?"

I groaned, covering my face. "It was wonderful! Of *course*, it was." I shook my head, smiling weakly. "He's... he's everything I hoped he would be."

The grin slid from my face as I thought of the night we'd shared. "After all this time, I just can't trust that any of it is real," I said.

Lucy looked like she was about to say something else, but we were interrupted by a short knock at the door.

Before we could respond, the door opened a crack, and a young woman with a tumble of chestnut brown curls peered through the gap. "C'mon, Luce! Stavrok's looking for you guys! Dinner's ready."

The newcomer tossed a grin my way.

I smiled back at her, a bit startled at the casual intrusion.

"I don't think we've met. You're the... sorceress, right?" the girl said.

Lucy rolled her eyes good-naturedly. "Marienne, this is Cass. Cass, Marienne."

One of the babies began to cry, so Lucy rushed to soothe her.

Cass bounded up to me, and she shook my hand within an inch of its life. "I've heard so much about you! I'm Stavrok's cousin. I guess you could say that makes me royalty, but mostly I'm just here for the free food."

I chuckled. "Well, I could eat."

"Stavrok says you guys have been all the way up north." Cass's eyes glowed with enthusiasm, and I couldn't help but follow her as she led me out of the room. "What's it like? Tell me everything."

I turned to Lucy, who now had a red-faced infant in her arms. "You two go along," she said. "I'll stay here for a while."

"See you later." I smiled at my friend as she sat down in a nearby rocking chair and offered her breast to her babe.

"I read that the north men all have pointed teeth—is that true?" Cass asked as she led me from the room.

"Um... I don't think so. Not that I saw, anyway." I shrugged. "But we weren't there for that long."

"Is the loner king really as fearsome as they say?"

"What *do* they say?" I asked, curious.

Cass shrugged. "That he never comes out of his castle in daylight. That he keeps feral wolves for pets. That his dragon is untamable, and many have died fighting it."

That didn't square with my impression of King Damon, but I didn't want to disappoint Cass, so I just made a noncommittal noise. She didn't seem to mind, and I let her talk nineteen to the dozen while we approached the dining room.

Lucy's words were running through my head on a loop. No matter how hard I tried, I couldn't stay present; they flooded my mind, leaving no room for anything else.

I've seen the way he looks at you, Mari. It's obvious how crazy you are about each other.

I wanted so desperately to believe her. But I couldn't let my own feelings cloud my judgment: I was the first to know that simply wanting something didn't necessarily make it true.

Erik sat beside me at dinner. I barely registered what I put in my mouth, much less tasted it. I was totally entranced by his mere presence. Everything about him caught my eye: his hair, the way he smiled, the heat radiating from him as the night wore on. Once, we brushed hands while reaching for the wine decanter, and the spark that shot through me was so potent I almost gasped out loud.

The others talked easily enough, but they seemed to chalk up my silence to exhaustion and left me alone for the most part.

That suited me just fine.

At some point, underneath the table, Erik's thigh brushed up against mine and stayed there for the rest of the meal. He continued to laugh and joke with Stavrok, looking for all the world like he was none the wiser about what he was doing to me.

The singular point of contact was maddening. I ached for him, deep inside my core.

"It seems like Mari's ready to call it a night." Stavrok winked at me over the top of his wineglass. "A toast! Without her, we wouldn't be any the wiser about King Damon."

Everyone raised their glasses toward me, and I flushed and looked down.

"I've had the servants prepare your rooms," Lucy said. "Please, make yourself at home!"

Hang on... rooms?

It occurred to me that I wouldn't be sharing a bed with Erik tonight.

Why was that so surprising? We'd agreed it wasn't like that between us.

So why does it feel like ice has lodged itself in my chest?

Lucy caught my gaze. If I didn't know any better, I would say there was a glint of amusement in her eyes.

She knew exactly what I was thinking.

I stood up so suddenly my knees knocked against the underside of the table. All the glasses clinked, and everyone looked up at me with surprise.

"Excuse me," I mumbled. "Stavrok's right. We have work to do tomorrow. I should get some rest."

I pushed back my chair and began to make my way across the dining hall. A clatter behind me echoed off the marble floor. I paused and looked back over my shoulder.

Erik was standing, staring after me. He was still at the table, but the look on his face was pure fire.

I exhaled softly and turned away, beginning the lonely journey up the steps of the great hall toward my lodgings. Frustration followed me all the way into the lovely bedroom waiting for me, like an ever-present itch beneath the surface of my skin.

I fell face-first onto the soft mattress with a groan. The release I craved was far beyond my reach.

As a matter of fact, he was likely still sitting downstairs, seeming totally in control of his body and his emotions, while I lay here growing ever more desperate.

After a few minutes of silent despairing, I got up and slipped into a sheer nightgown someone had left out for me, then padded around the room in the half darkness.

The excitement of the past couple of days thrummed through me. Sleep felt a million miles away. My mind turned over possibility after possibility for what the future could bring.

One image still haunted me: Erik lying in my arms, the life draining out of him before my eyes.

It couldn't be true. Surely, with knowledge, the future *could* change.

With a huff, I turned and crept over to the bed, sliding between the cool, soft sheets. The castle was quiet around me, dark and still. I didn't know what time it was, but it had to be close to midnight.

I lay in the silence, breathing. In, out. In, out.

This was no use. I'd never get any sleep tonight with all this uncertainty.

I flung a hand above my head to trace the carvings on the headboard. Even in the dark, I could guess their shape by touch alone. Flame, smoke, fury.

Dragon fire.

I sat up and pulled back the sheets. The fabric of my night-gown rustled against my calves as I dropped both feet to the floor and strode over to the door with renewed determination.

Erik didn't want me in a permanent way. Of that, I was pretty sure.

But I had to be certain. The look on his face at dinner tugged at something in my chest. I had no choice but to follow my instincts.

I reached out and grasped the heavy bolt on the door, sliding it free. The old oak shifted under my hands, and I pulled it open before I could talk myself out of going to find him.

My breath caught in my throat and I almost jumped back in fright.

Standing just beyond the door, with one hand outstretched, as if about to knock, was Erik.

I blinked at him. From the way his eyes flickered across my face, I knew a flush had spread across my cheeks.

"What are—" I began.

"I was just—"

We both stopped, hovering on the threshold, waiting for the other to finish their sentence. Without realizing what my body was doing, I swayed closer. His hot breath ghosted over the side of my neck, and I trembled.

My hands moved without my permission, grasping the front of his shirt. Beneath my fingers I could feel the hot, firm planes of his chest, rising and falling rapidly as if he had been running.

With a growl, he pushed forward, walking me back into the

room and tilting up my head. His mouth pressed against mine, and I opened for him with a moan of relief and desire.

I expected him to push me down onto the bed then, and have his way with me. I would have gone gladly.

But he didn't. His hand cradled the back of my neck, the other trailing down and sliding around my waist. He held me up against him, panting. His forehead pressed against mine. The intimacy was almost overwhelming; there was nowhere to look but straight into those burning eyes.

"I can't stand it, Mari." His voice, low and gravelly, made my stomach curl with heat. "I can't stay away from you."

I shook my head, hoping he understood; I was beyond words, beyond anything but the need that had me trembling, lips parted, aching for him to put his mouth on every part of me he could reach.

He cupped my face in his huge hands, holding me as if I was something precious to him. He kissed me again, soft and lingering, before angling us gently until I sat at the edge of the bed and he stood in between my open legs.

His hands inched up under the thin fabric of my nightgown. Even the slide of his fingers against the softness of my inner thighs had me squirming. In the dim light, I caught a flash of his crooked grin.

He leaned over me. His mouth found my cheek, the side of my neck, sliding hotly over my collarbone. He didn't seem to be in any hurry. The last time we did this, it had been relentless, inevitable; just pure, instinctual lust.

He was taking his time now. Mapping out my body, learning what made me gasp, what made me writhe and arch up against him. Slow and reverent.

No one had ever touched me like this.

No one had ever *seen* me the way Erik did.

He left a blazing trail up my inner thigh, closer and closer to where I really wanted him. Blindly, I reached out and slid a hand into his hair, anchoring him. He huffed as if in amusement, and my skin tingled at the sensation of his breath on me.

I groaned at the sight of his dark head buried between my thighs, and just barely managed to keep from crying out when he licked me, kissing around and over my clit while I bucked and rode up into his mouth like it was the only thing keeping me tethered to earth.

My other hand grabbed the head board, and his large palms slid under my thighs, pulling me impossibly closer. I lay there, trapped between his hot, damp mouth and the mattress beneath us. I could feel my climax approaching rapidly, and I squirmed, nudging at his broad back with my ankles to get his attention.

I didn't want it like this. I wanted to see him again, connect with him fully.

He glanced up. I shuddered at the wild look on his face, his mussed hair and wide pupils. I shifted beneath him, shuffling until I could wrap my hands around his huge forearms and guide him until he crawled up over me.

I leaned up and pressed a soft kiss against his mouth, heedless of where he had just been, and pushed his pants down his hips. I needed to feel his flesh against me.

He groaned as our kiss turned deeper, and our tongues slid together. My thighs trapped his pelvis against mine, and it wasn't long before his hips began sliding mindlessly downward.

Closer; closer. He got the message clear enough and reached down, taking his cock in hand and lining himself up. We both gasped when the head brushed against my entrance, and he slid inside slowly. I arched toward him, savoring the stretch and fullness of his organ inside my body.

I wrapped my hands around his shoulders, and pulled him down, pressing the length of his body against mine. He held himself rigid, clearly worried about crushing me under his weight, before relaxing into me. We rocked together, mouths brushing gracelessly against each other, lost to the world, and anything except the feel of each other.

His thrusts began to deepen. He growled against my neck, and I whimpered at the graze of his teeth against the skin there, tightening around him as my orgasm exploded through me. I gripped his jaw and dropped soft kisses onto his lips until he stiffened and roared. His cock pulsed with his own release deep inside me.

We both trembled as he withdrew and flopped down beside me on the bed.

I was utterly sated, wrung through with exhaustion and pleasure, but I smiled up at the canopy above us.

"What is it?" Erik murmured.

I turned my head to find he was studying me with a smile of his own.

I huffed a laugh, and his smile softened into a gentle grin. "It's just... I've been dreaming of you for so long."

Even in the darkness, I could see his eyebrows draw together. "Really?"

I reached out and pushed a loose strand of hair away from his gorgeous face. "Five years, in fact. Since the day I first saw you."

"So, you *did* see me that day," he murmured, turning fully onto his side and trailing a lazy hand through my hair, tangling it with his fingers. "You looked so beautiful, Mari, dressed in all your finery. I remember..."

"What?" I tilted back my head, allowing him to skim a hand over my collarbone.

He seemed caught up for a moment, lost in thought. "I'd never seen a woman so beautiful. And I knew that I'd never have you. We were so far apart... I thought the gods had cursed me. Set you in my path to punish me. I never stopped thinking of you, Marienne."

I inhaled sharply, catching his hand in mine and tangling our fingers together. "I'm sorry for all those years. All that pain." I sighed. "I wish it could've been different, Erik."

"The villagers whispered that you were a powerful sorceress," Erik mumbled, kissing my forehead, just below my tangled hair. "When I first saw you, I ran straight for the nearest field. I lost control completely... I shifted. I knew I had to get the hell away from the village, but I burned up an entire farmstead by accident. My mother was furious."

"Were *you* okay?" I stroked a hand down his bicep.

"Yes." He chuckled softly. "We had to pay for the damage for years, and no-one was hurt, but I thought you had *done* something to me. Some magic curse, or spell. I couldn't understand why my body reacted that way from just one look."

I wriggled closer, and he wrapped his long limbs around me. I sighed with satisfaction and rested my head on his chest.

"Well, I can assure you," I said with a smile, listening to the thud of his heart. "I'm just as much under your spell as you are under mine."

He pressed his face against my temple, and I felt his answering smile against my skin.

"I think I can live with that."

FOURTEEN

ERIK

After dozing, halfway between sleep and wakefulness for what felt like ages, I finally managed to open my eyes. I sighed deeply, contented. Marienne lay next to me, sound asleep, a warm comforting weight curled into my side.

Having her in my arms was perfect.

Just knowing that she felt the same way, after the doubt and turmoil of the last few days, was all I could ever have wished for.

As much as I wanted to stay here forever, we had to face what was coming for us. I couldn't stand aside and let Damon's kingdom fall because of his father's sins.

Stavrok felt the same way.

I glanced down to find Marienne awake. Her eyes were paler than usual in the morning light. The sun made their purple depths shimmer and sparkle, like the surface of a lake. Her expression was soft, but unsmiling.

It seemed I could now read her thoughts like a book. She was worried about me.

"I'll be fine." I stroked the side of her face. "The future can change, right? What you saw in that vision, it isn't set in stone."

She relaxed into my touch, but her eyes were still intent on mine.

"I'm going back there with you." She bowed her head, pressing a kiss onto my chest. It felt like a vow. "To the north."

Ice filled my veins. "It's not safe, Marienne."

Even as I spoke, I knew the words wouldn't change anything. It was just like last time. She had already made up her mind.

"I can help." Her voice was small, but firm. "I *want* to help."

I pulled her close against my chest. "I know," I murmured, cradling her against me. "I..."

The words that I wanted to say were on the tip of my tongue, but I couldn't let them out. It was too soon, too much. But I couldn't help how I felt.

I was falling in love with her.

So, I cut myself off, pushing the words back down and burying my face in her soft, sweet-smelling hair. Taking a few more stolen moments, before the world came crashing in again and destroyed our fragile, borrowed peace.

By the time we got downstairs, Stavrok and Lucy were waiting for us in the Great Hall.

"The troops are already on their way," Stavrok informed me, glancing at his wife. "Lucy's staying here with Cass and the babies. We should leave soon."

I nodded. Stavrok was wearing simple clothes, but his armor was piled up behind him. He followed my gaze and put a hand on my shoulder.

"This isn't your fight," he said. "Nor is it mine."

I had never fought in any kind of war before.

The memory of what I'd told Marienne last night resurfaced. My dragon, tearing through the countryside. Burning everything in its path, simply because I had spied a woman from afar. My shifter was strong, built for speed and stamina. I could do this.

"I know." I squared my jaw. "But we can't abandon the north, Stavrok. We can't abandon King Damon."

Stavrok's mouth twitched, and he shot me an approving smile. "Spoken like a true king." He turned his attention to Marienne, who had been watching our exchange with interest. "What about you, sorceress? Will you be joining us?"

Marienne inclined her head and her glance at me was warm. "My place is by my king's side, Your Majesty."

"Funny." Stavrok paused. "You used to say that when Magnik was alive. But now you actually sound like you *mean* it."

Marienne looked up sharply. Something passed between them, and I turned away. Stavrok clapped me on the shoulder, hard enough that I almost stumbled, then boomed with laughter.

"Better keep your wits about you, Erik." He winked at me. "There's steel behind those silk skirts, mark my words."

Marienne's eyes flashed, and she murmured something to Lucy. They both giggled.

"What is it?" I asked. Her voice had been too low, even for my astute shifter hearing.

Lucy turned to me, smirking. "She said, *he* should know. His wife is much the same, after all."

Stavrok scooped Lucy up by the waist with one massive arm, peppering her face with kisses while she squealed and tried half-heartedly to bat him away.

Something about their display of easy domesticity made me ache. Marienne met my eye, and in a flash, I could see that she was thinking the same thing.

The urge to lift her up and crush her against my chest in an embrace rose. I tried hard to tamp it down. I needed to concentrate on saving my energy for the coming flight.

The sun had already risen high in the sky by the time we set off. My shifter uncoiled itself lazily, sated after last night's activities but ready to fly nonetheless.

When I stretched out my wings, feeling Marienne's now-familiar weight settle onto my back, I almost relaxed. It felt like we'd done this a thousand times, her flying with me this way.

Stavrok flew by my side, dipping lower to skim through the cloud layer as we approached the Black Mountains. As I'd observed before, his dragon was bulkier than mine, with darker scales and piercing blue eyes as he turned his head back toward me. I made up for his bulk in wingspan, though, and I'd outpaced him by the time we flew over the mountain range into the northern territories.

We glided along, finding warmer air currents whenever we could, and I scanned the ground as we looked for signs of invasion. There was nothing amiss. Same sparse trees, same isolated little farmsteads, same snowdrifts.

Marienne's legs clamped tight against my back as she jerked. I turned my head, and my heart plummeted.

The small town outside the gates of Damon's castle was engulfed in flames.

Up ahead, dragons circled above the spires and turrets, locked in battle in the snowy sky. The enemy had already arrived. The castle itself appeared to be unharmed so far; its high stone walls and heavy drawbridge must have prevented the raiders from entering on foot.

Though by the ferocity of that attack, King Damon wouldn't be able to hold off the marauders forever.

I snapped out of my shock and refocused.

There wasn't time for distractions. I had to stick to the plan.

Soaring high above the castle, I circled, spotting a walkway where I could land safely. The moment my feet touched the battlements, Marienne slipped down off my scaly back.

She turned to look at me. Her eyes were full of unspoken

promises. There were a thousand things I wanted to say, but I couldn't shift back and speak to her. There wasn't time.

Go, she mouthed at me.

I didn't need telling twice. With one final look in which I poured everything I was feeling but couldn't say, I pushed off from the wall and soared into the air, ready to join the fray.

Marienne

That look. Even in his dragon form, I almost melted at the heat and promise in Erik's eyes. But there was no time to dwell on it.

I sprinted down the narrow, twisting hallway as fast as my legs could carry me, glancing out of every window I passed to see if the raiders had breached the walls.

So far, Damon's people seemed to be holding strong —for now.

I followed the corridors until I heard people—dozens and dozens of frightened voices—and then I followed those sounds, dashing past suits of armor and old tapestries until I reached a dimly lit, musty hall.

A group of people huddled in a corner close to the small fire. All of them looked up when I rushed in. As far as I could tell, the group mostly consisted of women and children. Every face held an identical expression of complete terror.

"Have you come to help us?" A sharp voice rang through the crowd.

I craned my neck until I identified the source: a young woman with the same pale, ice-blue eyes as King Damon.

I nodded. "I'm Marienne."

The woman visibly relaxed. She moved through the crowd, which parted easily to let her past. "Erik's queen? Damon said you'd come."

Erik's queen? I didn't correct her. Didn't want to. It sounded wonderful, even if it wasn't true.

"I'm Lenora, Damon's sister," the woman added.

"Nice to meet you." I glanced around, taking stock of the huddled mass of refugees. "Is this everyone from the town?"

Lenora looked grim. "Yes. All the women and children, at least. We managed to get as many people out as possible before… *they* came." A shadow fell over her face. "But there are more people coming from further afield. Farmers and such. They don't have anywhere else to go, but…"

She bit her lip, looking anguished. "I don't know how they'll make it through the battle and the raging fires outside, and get safely into the castle."

"Leave it to me."

I spread my fingers, letting a shimmer of my magic swirl out into the open air. Several people gasped; children hid behind their mothers and peeked at me, half-frightened, half-awed.

This was what I knew. The curse I was born with. The terrible gift that I could never escape. I would turn it around, and use it to help these people who were staring at me with little hope in their eyes.

Without another word, I whirled around and stalked to the huge window overlooking the outer walls of the castle. I murmured incantations and spread my arms wide. The magic flowed out, glimmering, sinking into the stonework, trickling down every nook and cranny.

Protective enchantments.

I had plenty of practice with them. Under Magnik's orders, I'd covered every inch of our castle with binding spells. It wouldn't keep out raiders forever, but it should at least slow them down.

A roar outside trembled the glass in the window opposite, and a jet of flame rushed past. Several people screamed.

I turned around, finding Lenora in the crowd, and beckoned

her over. "Keep everyone in here. Make sure they stay away from the walls, okay?"

"What?" Her eyes widened. "You're leaving?"

"You said there were people beyond the gates." I kept my voice soft and even, and placed a hand on her shoulder. "I'll help them if I can. You'll be safest in here. Bar the doors until you get my signal."

Lenora looked lost, but she nodded. There was a glint in her gaze, a semblance of steel behind the terror.

Good.

"Signal?" she asked. "What signal?"

I gave her a smile and, instead of answering, held out my palm and let the magic shimmer and dance across it.

"You really are a witch." Her eyes were round with amazement.

"I prefer sorceress." I shrugged. "And I'm going to use my magic to help as many of your people as I can." I didn't wait to hear her response. I hadn't come all this way to sit around in hiding. I had a job to do.

Erik

I FLEW HIGHER AND HIGHER, touching the misty underside of clouds as I banked and turned. Below me, the castle shrunk in size. I circled it, assessing the high walls for signs of weakness.

The battle raged below. Outside the burning town, our armies clashed with a ravenous mass of raiders.

There were fewer of them in number, but they made up for it in ferocity and skill. The air was thick with the clash of swords and the cries of the wounded. I skimmed lower, spread my wings, and soared down to take a closer look.

The enemy hordes were like something out of a nightmare. Vicious and bloodthirsty, they hacked through our armies with battleaxes wielded with deadly precision. In amongst them were huge, deadly wolves. They fought alongside the raiders like attack dogs, tearing into anyone they could get their jaws on.

I spotted Stavrok in the thick of the battle, wielding a broadsword. I couldn't fight like him. It was safer for me to stay in dragon form and help those of Damon's men in the sky.

Stavrok was in his element, though, if the fire in his eyes was anything to go by.

I pushed higher, rolling in the air, and flew to the top of the castle where two dragons scorched the skies with their fury.

As I watched, a paler one, which I assumed was King Damon, released an icy blue stream of fire, hitting his opponent square on the wing. The opponent roared with fury.

My stomach dropped as the other dragon barreled forward, catching Damon's wing in its claws and dragging him down toward the earth.

Damon struggled, but it was no use. He was plummeting to the ground at a speed impossible to survive if they impacted.

I didn't think twice. I shot through the air and crashed into the side of the enemy hard enough to force him to release Damon, and sent the raider hurtling down against the castle wall.

Damon twisted in midair and recovered himself, shooting upwards to join me. Together, we turned to face our adversary.

We didn't need words; one silent glance was all it took. We brought down the dragon together, like we had been fighting side by side for years. Brothers on the battlefield, bound by blood and fire.

Below us, the tide of the battle was turning. Our army was beginning to overwhelm the raiders, forcing them back through the burning streets of the town and out into the flat, barren wilderness.

I spied one small group of Damon's soldiers near the center of the fighting. They were cornered, but like trapped animals they were even more ferocious, baring their teeth at anyone who dared to come close. They were guarding the drawbridge.

My heart plummeted when I saw the reason why.

A huddled group of stragglers stood in the middle of the fray. Women and children. They were trying to head to the castle, but a pack of wolves prevented them from getting past.

I roared with fury and spread my wings wide, swooping down, all set to burn the raiders to the ground. But as I flew closer, I realized I couldn't risk the fire spreading or hitting innocent people with the force of my wrath.

A small figure appeared on the drawbridge. Slender and fragile against the massive stone walls behind her, she was surrounded by a glowing purple mist.

My heart froze. *Marienne? Oh, gods, she would be harmed if she stayed there.*

She reached the edge of the drawbridge, moving with slow, delicate purpose. The raiders froze, slack-jawed. Like moths drawn to her flame, they stepped closer and closer. The purple clouds wavered and trembled and the raiders began to twitch, shaking off her enchantment.

There were too many of them for Marienne to handle on her own. She began to back away as their large wolves advanced, slavering at the sight of their prey.

It was too much. I couldn't bear the thought of anything happening to Mari.

My roar split open the sky above us. The ground trembled, and everyone looked up.

Marienne was in danger, and I would level entire cities before I let any harm come to my mate.

The burst of my fire swept through the raiders and wolves, clearing a pathway edged with molten, glowing flames. The group of stragglers rushed toward Marienne, and she quickly ushered them over the bridge. Her magic cocooned them, protecting them from my fire. Her spell melded and fused together, sparking in strange and beautiful patterns. Working together in this strange yet wonderful way, we soon got everyone safely inside the castle.

The battlefield faded into the background. All I could see was Marienne, picking her way through the rubble and ruin, casting spell after spell to protect the castle and all those who sheltered inside.

I landed on the battlements. My dragon itched to get back into the fray, to burn, to *destroy*.

I wanted to kill every vile raider who had dared to threaten my mate.

With difficulty, I pulled back, calmed myself and focused my energy inwards, already feeling the air start to shimmer and morph around me.

I knew it was a risk, to walk through the heat of battle as Erik instead of in the safe body of my shifter. But I had to get down to the ground level. I needed to find Stavrok and Damon...

Ignoring my nakedness, I grabbed a sword from a fallen soldier and paced along the top of the battlements, eyeing the chaos that continued to rage outside the castle walls.

Below me, Stavrok staggered out of the fray. He sported a nasty-looking wound on his shoulder, but other than that appeared unharmed. I raised a hand to get his attention, and his eyes brightened. He climbed up the side of the wall like it was nothing, and I reached down and helped him the final few steps to safety.

Together, we stood watching the battle from our elevated vantage point. Stavrok was panting hard.

"Some fight, huh?" He turned to look at me, grinning.

I nodded. I had just opened my mouth to ask him what to do

next when he bellowed out a warning, lunging toward something just behind my left shoulder.

I didn't have time to react.

I felt rather than saw the axe blade that cut deep into my side. The pain was immediate, and excruciating. I twisted to face my attacker as he pulled his axe free.

His eyes... the hate-filled green. Those were the eyes of the dragon I'd taken down in defending Damon. I should have been more careful with his human half. I should have finished him off.

My attacker met the end of Stavrok's sword, but it was too late for me. The damage was already done. Marienne's scream pierced through the air. And then I collapsed to the ground.

❧

Marienne

MY LEGS THREATENED to fold out from under me. By some miracle, I managed to stagger closer to Erik, holding onto the wall for support as I went.

"No, *no. Erik!*"

I had been so close. I'd rounded the corner just a half-second too late.

Stavrok bellowed out a battle cry, tearing after the group of raiders who had managed to get past the castle walls. The lifeless body of Erik's attacker lay beside him.

I ignored the corpse, dropping to my knees, and tugged at Erik until his head was cradled in my lap.

This was my vision and it had come true. Nothing I had done today had changed the course of fate. And now I had to watch the man I loved die right before my eyes.

"Mari." Erik blinked up at me. His face was pale as ash, and he was clutching his side. He started to say something else, but broke away, coughing.

"Shh." I stroked back his hair, swallowing the tears that threatened to fall. "Shh. Erik, we did it. *You* did it. You were amazing."

He just stared up at me. There was a wonder in his eyes, like I was the most beautiful thing he had ever seen.

I pressed a hand against the crimson spot over his torso.

"No," I whispered, mostly to myself. "Not now. You don't get to leave me, Erik, you hear me? I have waited *too damn long* for you."

I squeezed my eyes shut, burning with grief and fury. Something was building inside me. My powers were coalescing, gathering, stronger than ever before. Fate may have brought us together, and I wouldn't let it tear us apart.

You don't get to take him from me! He's far too precious.

I threw back my head and let the power surge within me. Normally, I would dampen it down, keep it inside, afraid of what my magic would do if I let it free. But not this time. This time, I let go of my death grip and released my magic into the ether.

Wave upon wave of power pulsed out of me, pouring into the air. There were no incantations or rituals. No herbs or potions. No control. Just sheer, raw instinct, lighting up the atmosphere around us. The sky rolled with dark, thunderous clouds, and white lightning struck overhead. For an instant, I thought the entire castle would come crashing down.

I was beyond caring.

This was *Erik*, and he was dying in my arms.

I focused on him with every ounce of my willpower.

Don't die. I love you. Please, Erik. Please. Do. Not. Die.

The wind lashed at my face, and the magic kept on coming.

Then, just as suddenly as it had started, the surge was over. I slumped back onto the cold flagstones, completely and utterly spent.

Erik

D YING WASN'T AS painful as I'd once imagined it to be.

The world had taken on a dreamlike, hazy quality. Silver, and purple. My vision dimmed at the edges, then brightened and warmed. Marienne appeared, hovering over me like an angel.

I must be dreaming.

I didn't care. I wanted to reach up and touch her. She was so beautiful, so perfect. But I didn't have the strength to move.

I couldn't believe that, for a brief, shining moment in time, she had been mine.

Her lovely eyes were full of tears that threatened to spill down her cheeks.

No, that's not right...

She didn't have to worry about me now. I had given my life to save Damon's kingdom, but I knew I'd made the right choice. I couldn't have done anything else.

Mari's beauty pierced my soul. I could barely stand to look directly at her; she was like the sun, haloed by light, almost glowing with radiance. Except, there was no *almost* about it. She was *literally* glowing.

I wanted to raise my hand again, but I still couldn't move. She was so bright; *too* bright. The light engulfed her completely, and a searing, blinding pain shot through the wound in my side. I grit my teeth to stop from screaming out.

The light spread, unfurling in all directions, darkening the sky above us and making the very earth tremble beneath me. At the center of it all, Marienne's small frame swayed like a reed, right at the heart of the chaos she had somehow unleashed.

She looked strikingly vulnerable. It was too much. She was going to hurt herself, but I was powerless to help her.

At long last, the light faded, and it was over.

I gasped like a landed fish, taking in lungful after lungful of air and marveling at the lack of pain when I inhaled and exhaled.

Marienne slouched beside me. Her dark hair pooled to her waist, obscuring her face. Gently, I tucked a few strands behind her ear. Alarm bells rang in my head. Her skin was pale. Too pale. Her eyes were no longer the luminous, swirling mass of indigo blue-purple I had come to know so well. They were dull and magic-less. She looked up and met my gaze, smiling softly. I found her hand and squeezed it, trying not to show my shock at how cold she was to the touch.

"You're alive," she whispered. There was wonder in her tone.

I sat up, staring down at my side. My wound appeared to be healed. Her magic had put me back together. But what had it done to *her*?

"Can you walk?" I asked. I could hear the worry in my own voice, but she didn't seem to register it.

She nodded. "I... I think so."

Slowly, I helped her climb to her feet. She stood there, listing slightly to one side, and I darted in to slide a firm hand around her waist before she could keel over.

"Marienne." I pulled her close, pressing my fingers to her wrist to check her pulse. It was faint and irregular, but the sound of it reassured me. "What did you do?"

She reached up and touched my face. I turned my head and pressed a kiss into her palm, watching her eyelashes flutter at my touch.

"You saved me," she whispered. "I had to save you, too."

She made it sound so simple.

I wanted to yell, to tell her she'd been reckless. The truth was, it frightened me to see her like this. I didn't know what the power drain meant, if she would recover her energy. What if she'd weakened herself too much? What if…

I couldn't think it. I focused instead on what I *could* do: find the others.

The sounds of battle had grown fainter in the time we'd spent up here. It sounded like our forces had taken control of the situation.

Good.

I'd done all I could. Now it was time to take care of my own. I needed to take Marienne home.

FIFTEEN

ERIK

Eerie silence hung in the air around us.

The burnt-out shell of the town was utterly still. The blackened ruins of hollowed-out buildings were all that remained, some standing, most of them lying in piles of still-smoldering ash.

Thin, wispy trails of smoke were all that remained.

Most of the raiders were dead. The ones that survived had fled back toward the mountains.

Hopefully the raiders had gotten the message.

The northern clan is protected. The people will not pay for the old king's mistakes.

Damon surveyed the destruction with empty eyes. I could tell that he was thinking of the long road ahead. He would have to rebuild his kingdom from the ground up, repairing and restoring what had been lost.

Stavrok, Marienne, and I stood opposite him.

Out of the three of us, thanks to Marienne, I was the only one who had emerged unscathed from the fight.

Stavrok was gritting his teeth and clutching a nasty shoulder wound. It wasn't life-threatening, thank God.

More worryingly, Marienne clung to my side like I was the only thing keeping her standing. Which I likely was. I had to pay my respects to Damon, but I needed to take her away from this place. Soon.

"I can't express how grateful I am to you," Damon said. "All of you. I vow one day to repay your kindness."

"Let this be a new chapter in our realm's history." Stavrok spoke slowly, letting every word hang in the air. "An alliance to last for generations to come."

We shook hands, and I gripped Damon's arm when it came to my turn.

"Any manpower, supplies, building materials you need…" I trailed off, surveying the frozen landscape around us. "You shall have them."

Damon's eyes flickered with gratitude, and he nodded. His attention turned to Marienne.

"You must get her home, Erik," he said softly. "As much as I appreciate your help, don't hang around on my account."

I squeezed Marienne's hand, and she gave a faint squeeze in response. "I know."

"I would offer you the use of my castle, but I'm afraid it's not fit for purpose right now." Damon glanced up at the huge mass of stone behind us. "My people need me."

"Can you fly?" I asked Stavrok, and he gave me a nod.

"It's a flesh wound. I've had worse." He shot me a sharp grin, and then wandered away. He glanced at us behind his shoulder just before he turned the corner of a nearby, smoke-blackened wall. "May we all meet again soon."

He shifted into his dragon form and flew away.

My mind was already on the logistics of getting Marienne home safely. She couldn't ride on my back. She wasn't strong enough.

"I'll carry you," I murmured into her hair. "We're going home, Marienne."

The journey seemed to last a lifetime. I carried Marienne in my talons, imagining the flutter of her heartbeat. She felt impossibly small and fragile. I flew as fast as I dared, but every flap of my wings felt like hours too long. I exhaled in relief when the mountains appeared on the horizon.

The sky was clearer than it had been in days. The snow had stopped falling, and a beautiful sunset streaked across the sky.

I thought about the raiders in the mountains, and the wilderness we had just left behind. Would we ever return?

My chest twinged with relief when we passed over the mountains. On the other side, the valleys rolled out in shades of green and blue, warm and inviting.

Familiar. We were home.

I drifted to the top of the nearest tower, setting Marienne down as gently as possible. The servants ran out to greet us. Thomas took the lead, carrying a robe for me.

Good man.

I shifted quickly and threw on the robe before hurrying over to Marienne. She was on her feet, at least.

I took her slender shoulders and gazed down at her. She smiled, her eyes tracking over my face as if she were trying to commit it to memory.

Then the last of her energy seemed to leave her. She let out a deep sigh, and her body sagged against mine.

"Marienne?" I held her against me, as tightly as I dared. I slid my hands into her hair and turned her face up to mine. "Mari, please..."

Her eyes were closed. She was so cold.

I fell to my knees, pulling her down with me. I could feel the servants hovering around me, but I paid them no mind. Nobody dared to come near us.

My shout echoed through the mountains, and into the valleys below. "Marienne!"

Marienne

THE FIRST THING I registered was warmth, and softness.

I stirred. In my half-conscious state, confusion filled me. I didn't remember falling asleep. It was all a blur. The last thing I remembered was...

Oh.

My eyes snapped open.

A gauzy canopy filled my vision. I blinked up at it, trying to put the pieces together in my mind.

I'm in the master suite bed again? How did I get here?

I shifted. Warm fingers curled around my hand, outstretched across the covers. I turned my head on the pillow and smiled.

A chair had been pulled up at the side of the bed. Erik sat, slumped over with his face against the mattress. His hair had fallen over his face. He was dozing. Both of his huge hands cradled mine.

Moving slowly, I extracted my hand. My fingers reached out and carded through his hair, brushing it back. He stirred.

He sat up, blinking a few times. His eyes were shadowed. He looked like he hadn't slept for a long while.

"Hey," I whispered, and his face broke into that crooked grin I'd come to love so much.

"You're awake." Relief flooded his face as he looked over me.

"How long was I out?"

"Too damn long." He huffed a laugh, shaking his head in disbelief. "Couple of days."

"Days?" I grimaced and then relaxed back into the pillows. My head still tingled; I sensed that getting up wasn't the best idea right now. "Did I miss anything good?"

He laughed again, before glaring at me. "Other than me almost losing it because I thought you were *dead?* Not much."

"What?" I reached out and took his hand, forcing him to look at me.

"These past two days…" He broke off, clenching his jaw. "It made me picture what it would be like to lose you."

I wanted to say something, to interject. I didn't.

"I don't want to rule, Marienne," Erik said, lowering his gaze, "unless you're by my side."

"Oh," I breathed.

He drew up my hand and pressed a kiss there as he continued.

"I love you. All of you. I never want you to change, Marienne, and I never want you to leave. Stay with me." He slid to his knees, keeping a gentle grip on my hand as I peered over the bedside, amazed. "*Marry* me."

I froze, astounded. After everything we'd been through together, everything he'd seen, Erik still wanted me. *He wants to marry me!*

He didn't care about my past, or the strength of my magic.

This man—this wonderful, ridiculous man—wanted me. For *me.*

"I—" I stopped, joy spilling over in my chest. "Yes. I'll marry you."

His whole expression lit up, and he launched himself onto the bed, careful not to jostle me. His eyes shone with happiness when I cupped his face in my hands.

"You will?" He grinned at me. "Say it again."

"Yes," I repeated, laughing. "Of *course,* I'll marry you!"

I squealed when he dived in and kissed me, over and over in spite of my protests.

After all, I didn't put up *too* much of a fight.

EPILOGUE

MARIENNE

"I have been married *before*, you know," I said to Lucy as she clucked over me like a mother hen.

Behind me, in the mirror of my dressing table, Lucy's eyes rolled in exasperation. We were sitting in my new bedroom. Erik's room.

"I know, but not to someone you actually—"

"Love?" I smirked.

"Exactly." Lucy held up two heavily jeweled tiaras and I turned to face her.

I wrinkled my nose at them, and she let out a sigh.

"These are traditional! I got them out of the Treasury. They are meant for a queen. And you *are* a queen." She brushed a loose strand of hair over my shoulder, and I couldn't help but smile at her. "You're going to be the Queen of the Black Mountains, Marienne! For *real* this time."

I eyed the tiaras, trying to keep an open mind.

Nope, I was right the first time. They're still hideous.

My gaze drifted past Lucy, to the elaborate floral arrangement on the table behind her. Sprigs of white flowers clustered together, interspersed with pale lilac and gold.

"Screw tradition," I said, standing up and arranging my dress behind me. "Let's do something different."

Lucy raised an eyebrow, and then caught on to my train of thought.

She smiled broadly. "Ah. Yes, I think that will work."

My hand curled protectively over my belly, and I smiled.

It had turned out that conceiving with my fated mate was simpler than I ever thought possible. Whether Magnik was infertile, and blamed it on me instead, or he didn't know... none of it mattered now.

I'd thought I was the problem, and that my magic refused to allow me to grow a child. But instead, I had just needed the right man. *My* man. My fated mate.

I wasn't showing yet, but that wouldn't last for long. Nobody knew except Erik and I that we were expecting. We planned to announce it at the wedding reception.

Things between me and my soon-to-be husband hadn't gone the way everyone expected they would.

They'd turned out even better.

Erik

I GAZED out over the crowd of onlookers, trying not to let the nerves show on my face.

The hall was as busy as it had been on my coronation day. I thought back to that moment, standing here in a sea of strangers with no idea of what lay ahead.

The memory made me smile, now. Such a short time, and yet so much had changed.

The wedding preparations had been simple. Neither of us wanted a huge show.

We had other things on our mind.

Ruling my own kingdom took priority, but I spent time in the north when I could afford to spare it, traveling up with Stavrok and checking in on Damon to see how the rebuilding efforts were going.

His father's debtors had been scared off for good by our alliance. Pride and happiness filled me when I thought of how much we'd achieved in such a short period of time.

Speaking of which...

I grinned to myself, thinking of the news that Marienne and I had to share later tonight.

"Something on your mind, my friend?" Stavrok's voice startled me out of my thoughts. I glared at him, and he promptly burst out laughing. "Stop scowling! You have plenty to smile about. You're marrying your fated mate, Erik. Not many people get to say that."

My scowl instantly cleared. I could hardly believe it myself.

It had taken me a long time to trust that I was worthy of someone like Marienne. But we fit together, flaws and all.

"It could have ended very differently," I reminded Stavrok, as well as myself.

His face darkened.

"Indeed." He pointed at me, looking stern. "You—you need some sparring practice, my friend."

"Hey, I know!" I held up my hands and burst out laughing. "You won't hear any complaints from me on that front!"

If I had to go a few rounds in the castle courtyard with a training master to ready myself for battle one day, I would. But I couldn't think about that today.

My gaze wandered down the aisle and flickered through the rows of guests, all decked out in their finery. All the kingdoms were here. Cass was sitting in a nearby row and I smiled at her.

She grinned back, before catching sight of Stavrok and sticking her tongue out at him.

"Hey Stavrok, have you considered taking Cass up to the northern kingdom?"

Stavrok drew his eyebrows together. "No, why?"

I grinned at him, having heard from Marienne that she'd had a premonition the day she'd shaken Cass's hand. The young girl had been interested in knowing more about the castle to the north, and Marienne believed Cass would do well up there.

"Damon's still looking for his fated mate, and Marienne suggested to me that you might want to take Cass along on your next visit up there."

Stavrok's eyes widened a little. "But, she's only nineteen."

I shrugged. "Then wait a year or two. I'm sure Damon's not going anywhere."

Stavrok nodded once, though his jaw was tight with sudden tension and indecision. I'd wanted to impart that knowledge to him for months, and it was a burden I was grateful to now shift onto his shoulders.

The winter king had sent his congratulations, but he'd declined our invitation to attend. I understood; he had his hands full for the foreseeable future. If the loner king ever did decide to venture south, at least he knew he had friends waiting for him.

On the other side of the aisle, my new councilors sat whispering amongst themselves. They included representation from all over the kingdom: both the town, and the outlying countryside. One of them, my butler Thomas, caught my eye and nodded his head respectfully.

There was not a single gold chain to be seen among them. I smiled to myself.

I hope the old elders are keeping themselves warm with their gold, now that they are no longer welcome in my castle.

Stavrok leaned in again, and I turned toward him.

"Word has it that you're quite the natural statesman," he said. "If the rumors from my wife are to be believed."

"That's all Marienne." I shrugged. "I can't claim any credit. I couldn't have done it without her."

"I'm sure she'd say the same about you."

I shot Stavrok a grateful smile. I had chosen the right guy to be my best man today.

The hall began to fill with the sounds of soft, ethereal music, and the double doors swung open. My heart clenched with nerves and anticipation.

It was finally time.

Mari stood there, haloed by sunlight. I couldn't keep the smile off my face. Her dress floated and swirled around her, and her perfect face was framed by dozens and dozens of flowers.

She had a whole crown of them. They tumbled through her long hair, their tendrils trailing through her veil, the latter held up by a smiling Lucy. As she walked along the aisle, the whole room seemed to come alive in her wake.

I almost forgot to breathe. She looked like a goddess.

The tension in my shoulders drained away, and my heart warmed. Meeting Marienne's gaze, all I felt was peace, and certainty about the future.

This was just the beginning.

THE END

~

CHAPTER

ONE

DAMON

"Sire." The voice of my chief advisor startled me out of my thoughts. "They're here."

I straightened and stood up from my throne, striding forward into the center of the room. It was customary to greet a fellow king on equal ground. I could not meet my guests from high on my throne.

The formal clothes I wore were stiff and uncomfortable. I much preferred to wear my everyday attire, but my advisors had cautioned against it. I found all the court rules and regulations stifling, especially when my mind and my focus was on the repair work I'd been carrying out with my men this morning.

Still. Stavrok had shown me great generosity during the battle by coming to our aid. Not to mention what he'd done for us since we started repairing. It was only fitting that I return that favor by allowing him and his cousin to visit and see the renovations.

Plus, it gave me a chance to show the other kingdoms that we were slowly regaining our former strength. My ancient house—the family of ice dragons that had ruled the north for generations—had survived the raiders.

The castle wasn't the only thing my father had driven to ruin. I needed to rebuild alliances, treaties. And the best way to do that was to ensure peace with my fellow rulers.

The corners of my mouth lifted into a polite, welcoming smile as the doors opened.

"His Majesty, King Stavrok of the Bravdok Clan, and his cousin, the Princess Cassandra."

Stavrok strode into the room with all the brazen confidence I remembered. The years since the battle hadn't changed him that much; only a few more threads of silver in his hair indicated that time had passed.

I greeted him with a nod, and he grinned back, charging over with his hand outstretched, ready to pull me into a friendly bear hug.

He only managed to get halfway to me, however, before I caught sight of the other newcomer standing behind him.

My dragon woke from its slumber, uncoiling inside my chest. I gasped, trying to push him down.

Something I'd never felt before pulsed through my veins, dark and hot, filling me with a single-minded purpose: a *desire* like I'd never known before.

What the hell is this?

Whatever it was, I had no power to stop it.

My vision began to change. Everything in the room faded out of focus. And nothing else mattered. Not my kingdom. Not my castle repairs. Not the fact that I was a king.

Only *she* remained.

Her chestnut brown hair hung in loose curls, dusted with snowflakes from her journey. Her eyes were wide and fringed with dark lashes. Unlike most of the shifters I had met, who all had icy, pale blue eyes, hers were a deep, warm brown.

I need her.

The realization hit me like an anvil. I didn't know what it

meant. And I didn't have time to work it out. I strode forward, my gaze zeroed in on my prize.

Stavrok stepped in front of her, blocking my path. He knocked away my hands outstretched for her. I let out a deep growl, prepared to shift if I needed to fight the other man. My neighboring king.

Stavrok was on the brink of fighting as well. I caught sight of his dragon when his angry gaze flashed to meet mine. Hot rage curled within me and I lowered my stance. Stavrok would not keep her from me.

She wasn't any woman. This one was mine.

I knew the difference. I'd had women before. I was a dragon king, and I had to satisfy my appetite for pleasure alongside everything else.

The stresses of recent years meant I'd tamped down my desire. In the face of all I had to build, a fumble with a maid or some woman in town felt like a waste of time. I had responsibilities, more important things to deal with than my sex drive.

Not that countless women hadn't put themselves in my path on purpose. I was their king. More often than not, I'd rebuffed them.

And this was why. *She* was why.

All thought of polite pleasantries and formal introductions were long gone. Stavrok and I circled each other, Stavrok keeping himself between me and the girl as I snarled with impatience.

We weren't two kings anymore, ready for an official royal visit. This was deeper. Primal.

We were dragon shifters and the need to fight this invader, this intruder in my kingdom, coursed through me as strong as the ocean.

For whatever reason, the mere sight of this girl inflamed my dragon like no other.

Only one thing remained: the feral, frenzied, uncontrollable urge to take her and carry her out of here.

Stavrok shouted something, but I was too far gone to hear it. I could only watch, burning with fury, as he grabbed the girl by the arm and practically dragged her out of the room.

The moment the heavy door thudded closed behind them, I was at the door, pounding against the wood. My shifter writhed in frustration; it was all I could do not to release my anger, shift, and burn down my own door to get to her.

"Stavrok!" I bellowed, fists balled against the immovable oak door. "Open the door, right now!"

"So, it is true," the voice came back, muffled, from the other side of the door. "Marienne was right."

I was losing patience. As every minute passed, shifting looked like a more and more appealing plan.

"What is true?"

"You're my cousin's true match. Her fated mate," Stavrok yelled through the door.

I forced myself to take deep, ragged breaths, fighting to regain control. It was easier now that the girl wasn't in the same room, but knowing exactly where she was, just out of reach... the feeling of it, the knowledge... It was pure torture. I groaned.

"The two of you are destined for each other."

I pressed my forehead against the door, growling. "Then what are you waiting for? Let me through!"

"You're not in control, Damon!"

I bared my teeth at him, unseen. Frustration pounded through me.

"She's young..." Stavrok hissed. "And still a virgin!"

"Stavrok!" Another voice cut in. A sweet, light voice, admonishing him for revealing a truth that had my dragon retreating slowly.

I straightened when I heard her voice, crowding as close as possible up against the door, hoping she would speak again.

"Get yourself together," Stavrok said. "I'm warning you. If you can't control your dragon, I will leave, and I'll take Cass with me. You'll never see her again."

He sounded dangerous, deadly. If I were in my right mind, I would have been afraid. Stavrok was a fearsome warrior. I had no doubt that if anything happened to his beloved cousin, he would have my head for it.

I focused on breathing, clearing the fog that had spread through my senses.

"Okay." I took a few steps back from the door. "I'm ready."

～

You can DOWNLOAD book 3 here:
https://books2read.com/u/3Ly8MN